According to R.
were dating the au
book when she first [started, though]
it made to much sense to give this
as a final gift. PLEASE read this and
tell me how it is! - CLowe

MW01265401

I hope this book is both enlightening
and insightful. May it remind you
of us and move you to visit.
(I have no idea what this book is about so
maybe it is any of those things. Probably
not though)
          - CJ

The Vulture Circles

Copyright © 2023 by Chris Gallagher

All rights reserved.

Permission to reproduce or transmit in any form or by any means, electronic or mechanical, including photocopying, photographic and recording audio or video, or by any information storage and retrieval system, must be obtained in writing from the author.

The Vulture Circles is a registered trademark of Chris Gallagher.

First printing August 2023

Library of Congress Cataloging-in-Publication Data

Gallagher, Chris

the vulture circles / by chris gallagher

Paperback ISBN: 9798852790057
Hardcover ISBN: 9798858243014

Published by AR PRESS, an American Real Publishing Company
Roger L. Brooks, Publisher
roger@incubatemedia.us
americanrealpublishing.com

Cover design by: Ryan Vanderbeek and Roger Harvey

Edited by: Margaret Bendet

Printed in the U.S.A.

THE VULTURE

CIRCLES

Chris Gallagher

ACKNOWLEDGMENTS

No book is the work of just one person. I would like to express my heartfelt gratitude to those whose inspiration and support made possible the completion of this novel.

I'll begin with my wife, Britta Turney, who was my first sounding board. Her honest feedback helped shape the initial rough story into the finished book it is today. And since this is a series, she's not off the hook yet.

The book is dedicated to our incredible son, Lucas Gallagher, and was brought into the world on his tenth birthday. Lucas's smile and wit have long kept me grounded and motivated to succeed. I wanted this book to demonstrate to Lucas that each of us has the power to bring magic into the world. In fact, Lucas isn't much older than I was when I was first inspired to write.

With that in mind, let me also acknowledge the kind and steady support of Debbie Farrell, my fourth-grade teacher, whose encouragement and belief in my writing abilities planted a seed of passion that has taken form as this novel. Mrs. Farrell instilled in me a love for storytelling.

I am also appreciative of the dedicated professional support I received from my editor, Margaret Bendet, whose wordsmithery and keen eye for detail transformed my story into a polished piece of work.

And, last by not least, I am grateful to the artists Ryan Vanderbeek and Roger Harvey for creating cover art that captures the essence of my story and brings it to life in an image. I didn't know it could be done!

To all my family, friends, and readers who have supported me on this journey, thank you for your belief in me and your enthusiasm for my work. Your encouragement has fueled my determination to tell my stories.

The Vulture Circles would not have been possible without the contributions of each and every one of you. From the bottom of my heart, I thank you.

.

"Men are what their mothers made them." – Ralph Waldo Emerson

CHAPTER ONE

The concept of time is irrelevant when all things are eternal. I finally understand what he meant by that and through the pain, I've learned to accept it. I'm here now, and this is all I know. I'm driven to find the truth and some semblance of peace. Perhaps when I find what I'm desperately searching for, time will have meaning again.

When I first arrived, I was terrified, and every emotion has run through me since. I've been sad, angry, scared, and—much to my surprise—there have been brief moments of happiness, but the guilt is constant and well deserved. Actions have consequences, but little did I know my infidelities would lead to my death.

"Oh my God, what time is it?" I rose in a panic, frantically gathering my clothes.

"What? Maggie, come back to bed," a groggy Brent leaned over, caressing my leg as I pulled up my panties.

"Are you crazy? It's 1:00 a.m. Look," I showed him my phone. Five missed calls from Cliff and multiple text messages.

"Oh shit, me too!" Brent's wife, Melissa, had called ten times and texted the same amount, starting with concern but ending with suspicion.

"I have to go." I gave Brent a kiss and darted out the door of room 212 at the Comfort Inn.

My heart was pounding as my alcohol-laced blood pulsed through my body. I hoped to make it home without getting pulled over, as otherwise, I'd no doubt be spending the night in jail for drunk driving. The thought actually went through my mind to purposely get pulled over. A DUI would cover up this latest slipup in the affair with Brent that had started over a year ago.

We had become quite brazen lately, and tonight's debacle would surely be the end of both of our marriages. The night had started out as a birthday gathering for one of my girlfriends. Brent and I texted throughout the evening, as he was out with his buddies, too. Our plan to meet up at the motel was hashed out after we were both intoxicated, although we probably would have made the same, stupid decision sober. We were out of control, and the thrill of being bad had taken over. We didn't love each other, but we loved the rush, the sex and everything else that came with sneaking around.

I made it home safely just after 1:30. To my surprise, Cliff was not waiting up for me. He was sleeping soundly when I tiptoed into our room. I wreaked of alcohol and sex. I couldn't simply cozy up to him like this. I took a shower in the guest bathroom to wash the guilt off of me. If only it were that easy. I looked at myself in the mirror after I got out of the shower, wondering how it had come to this. Cliff and I used to be the envy of our friends. Up until Brent, Cliff was the only man I'd been with. We were supposed to have lasted forever, but the fairy tale of our high school sweetheart romance had come crashing to the ground—and I was the one to blame. I went to bed without waking him. It seemed the least I could do for him now. My head was spinning as I fell asleep.

"I'm taking the kids to church." Cliff nudged me a few times on my shoulder to make sure I heard him. "We'll see you when we get back. You and I can talk then."

"No, I'll go. I'll go." I popped up in bed, trying to gather myself, my head still pounding from the ill-advised tequila shots.

"Maggie, we're walking out the door. Forget it." Cliff walked out of the room, yelling for the kids to get in the car.

I grabbed a Goody's headache powder from our bathroom drawer, poured the nasty stuff into the back of my throat, and gulped down a full glass of water. Hangovers like this were rare for me. A text came through on my phone. It was Brent, although the name on the display said Brenda. I was Michael on his phone—and, more importantly, to his wife. Brent wanted to call me and was asking for an all clear. I replied with an "OK."

"What did Melissa say?" I asked.

"She was pissed, but I told her I got too drunk and crashed on Paul's couch until I felt like I could drive home." Brent sounded nonchalant about what I perceived to be last night's disaster.

"She bought that?" I never would have accepted that story from Cliff.

"Yeah, relax. She bought it. What about you?"

"I don't know. They left for church before we could talk. He said he wants to talk when he gets back." Thinking about the looming

2

confrontation made me feel panicky.

"You'll be fine. Use my story. It'll work." Brent was arrogant, stupid, or both.

I started in on him. "We should have just met at the motel like we planned. Why did you come to the bar? That was fucking stupid. People who know Cliff and who know Melissa saw us leave together. I'm sure of it." I had finished my first cup of coffee and was ready to down another. I never drank more than one cup a day.

"Really? You asked me to come, remember?"

Brent was right. In my happy inebriation, I'd suggested he stop by. Stupid. "I have to go," I told him. "We need to take a break. I need to figure this out."

I did this all the time. I'd get scared and push Brent away only to go right back to him after a few days.

"OK, I got it." Brent wasn't worried. He knew it wouldn't be long before we were back together.

The Suburban pulled into the driveway. The kids got out first—Ben, Christopher, and Todd, along with the only girl, the youngest, Reese. Cliff got out last.

Ben, who had just turned seventeen and had recently passed his driver's test, was the first in the door. He said, "Dad let me drive both ways today."

"Yeah, let's not do that again," Todd, our twelve-year-old smart-ass, chimed in.

Reese asked me, "Mommy, are you sick?" Apparently, that was Cliff's story to cover my absence at church.

"I'm feeling better now, baby." My head did feel better from the Goody's, but the rest of me was a wreck. The anticipation was killing me.

Cliff stepped in, saying, "Ben, why don't you and Chris help get breakfast started." Cliff walked toward our bedroom, and I followed.

After I closed the bedroom door, I offered my apologies right away. "Before you say anything, I'm sorry Cliff. I'm so sorry."

"What the fuck were you doing last night, Maggie?" Clearly, Cliff had been bottling up his anger since last night.

"I know, I know, I screwed up. I'm sorry. The night got out of hand." I couldn't look him in the eye.

"One-thirty in the morning, Maggie, really! Where were you?" He was focused on suspicion rather than concern, or at least that's how it felt.

"We were at McKenzie's until just before midnight, and then the girls wanted to head over to Monica's for a bit." McKenzie's is a local place that Cliff and I frequented. He knew how close it was to Monica's house.

"Yeah, and?"

"And I passed out on her couch. I'm sorry, I overdid it." I had the audacity to raise my voice and go on the offensive.

"The kids don't know that you came home so late. Let's keep it that way. You're an embarrassment." Cliff went to the kitchen then; he closed the bedroom door on his way out.

I wasn't naive enough to think that Cliff bought my lame story. The truth was that he didn't care anymore. If it weren't for the kids, we'd never speak to each other. Our once happy marriage had devolved into a robotic relationship that was about paying the bills, getting the kids to their events on time, and the occasional holiday celebration that would provide the appearance that everything was OK.

Sunday came and went, but I didn't feel any better. Brent didn't abide by my imposed break. He texted me throughout the evening. I kept deleting them.

Monday brought us back to our family routine. It was summertime; therefore, the kids were each involved in their various camps or working. Ben had a part-time gig at Home Depot, Christopher was taking a summer course on robotics at school, Todd was playing serious baseball, and Reese had dance camp. Cliff had started a contracting business about ten years before, and was making a success of it. I was proud of him. I was proud of both of us. Juggling four kids and a business is no easy task. It's hard to imagine, but I guess I got bored, and Brent was just a convenient distraction. He provided a thrill in my rather mundane lifestyle.

I never dreamed that my poor choices would lead to a tragedy and would put Franklin, Tennessee on the map for all of the wrong reasons.

CHAPTER TWO

Tuesday, July 26, was one of the hottest days on record in Franklin with the temperature going all the way up to 103 degrees. Cliff was on a job site, and I, as usual, found myself at home alone. I had barely slept since Saturday night. The stress of this affair was taking its toll. Brent continued to text and call me, and, before long, I caved in. Melissa and their kids had gone to visit her parents in Knoxville. They'd be there through the weekend. Brent was going to meet them in Knoxville on Friday night.

I saw Brent at his house, as we had done from time to time when his family was out of town. Being with Brent was the first time I'd felt normal since Saturday. While that doesn't make much sense, it was the way I felt. My stress completely disappeared for the few hours we were together, and it returned as soon as I left his house. That encounter turned out to be the last day we spent ruining our marriages. It was the last day not because we suddenly found morals. It was the last day because it was the last day of my life.

Cliff and I made sure the kids were asleep one-by-one. Reese, the earliest to bed around 9:00 p.m., and Ben, the latest, around 10:00. Cliff and I watched TV in silence with the weekend's events still fresh in both our minds. I specifically remember the House Hunters episode that I dozed off to. The couple was moving to St. Louis, and they were just about to choose the house they wanted out of the three finalists, but my eyes proved too heavy. The stress of the last few days finally caught up to me, and I drifted off to sleep. I never saw which one they chose.

The rampage started at approximately 11:45 p.m. and ended with what would be the most horrific crime scene in Franklin's two hundred-plus years. Rage and a claw hammer. It took only one blow to my skull

5

to kill me, but just to be sure, I was bludgeoned fifty-three times all over my body with a special focus on my private area. The crime scene team had a feeling it was me laying there in a pool of blood on the bed, but they could only know for sure by checking my dental records. That's how vicious it was.

The kids suffered because of my actions too. The details are too gruesome to share, and why would anyone want to hear about those details anyway. Although, it hasn't stopped the hoard of media that's been camped out on our street since the news broke. Nancy Grace and her cronies are having a field day with this one. Reese, Christopher, and Todd were next. All were asleep, and they suffered the same fate as me. Two blows to each of their skulls was all it took. The rage wasn't as powerful, no need to strike them fifty-one more times each. He covered their faces with their blankets, just like the coward he is. He couldn't look at what he had done.

Ben made it. Unbelievably, Ben made it out alive. His survival didn't come without consequence. His shoulder was hit badly. The claw almost made it down to the bone. He got his licks in on Cliff, too; they were both a bloody mess. My boy fought hard and avoided becoming the fifth casualty. Instead, he became the only witness to the attacks, not that the investigators necessarily needed one. They've seen these domestic disputes time and time again, though never to this level. Who did it and the motive were clear as day. Cliff will have to answer to the law there on Earth, but more importantly face consequences in the afterlife.

The afterlife is something that I've gotten to know all too well. I've been here a long time, but like I've been told before, the concept of time is irrelevant when all things are eternal. When I arrived here, I attempted to keep track of my days, but I learned that there's no such thing as "days." The playing field is completely different here, and it only vaguely resembles anything I was taught in church for all those years. The devil, God, Heaven, Hell, that's all fine and good, but it's not reality. Reality, for me, was having my skull crushed and the life taken out of me, and not just physically. I had been taught that I'd go to Heaven to be with my loved ones. Not only have I not seen my loved ones, I haven't even seen my most important loved ones, my children. Dealing with this "in between" world would be much more tolerable if I had my kids with me. Mentally, I'm dying all over again.

Those first moments after I arrived are burned into my brain. I was helpless and scared. When I first opened my eyes and looked up to the sky, I could feel my heart beating in my chest. I was on my back and just short of hyperventilating when the panic set in. I jerked my head side-to-side only to find what appeared to be wheatgrass all around me. For some reason I was wearing an old, ratty dress that I remember having when I was a teenager. I'd hated it then, and I hated it even more now. I brought my head back to center and looked up again to find three birds circling above me. A calming sensation came over me as I looked closer to discover that these were vultures. That may seem odd, that these creepy looking scavengers helped calm me down, but I've always been fascinated by vultures and their role in the cycle of life.

I don't recall how long I was staring at them or why they brought me a sense of peacefulness in this uncertain situation, but it was mesmerizing almost to the point of paralysis. It may have been minutes, or possibly hours, that I stared at them circling. I had no reason to believe these vultures were here for me, so I didn't fear them. They were about a hundred feet above me and equidistant from one another in a perfect circle that appeared to be about a hundred feet in diameter. Each bird would occasionally flutter its wings a couple of times and then glide around the circle, never losing the perfect distance they had created between themselves. They continued to circle directly overhead. I knew that when vultures are circling it usually means a carcass of some sort is close by.

Slowly, I began to sit up. It was time to get moving. I had no idea where I should go or what I should do, but I knew staring into the sky wasn't going to accomplish anything. I figured there must be a dead animal close by. I had no idea what or who had killed it. I took another glance at my ratty dress, shook my head in disgust, and rose to my feet. The next time I looked up again, the vultures were gone. I looked all around, but they had vanished.

As my line of vision lowered back down to the horizon, I began to turn around in a circle. Everything looked exactly the same for miles. It was wheat fields as far as I could see, just about three feet off of the ground and stretching in all directions. The sun was about to set, producing my elongated shadow, which stretched about fifteen feet from where I was standing. I tried to remain calm with the curiosity and beauty of the moment serving as a nice distraction.

I had always been a church-going person, but I never considered myself overly religious. I prayed regularly and found my prayers to be cathartic and felt like God answered them most of the time. There were plenty of times that I didn't like the answer, but at least I had some kind of closure. In a moment like this I figured prayer couldn't hurt, and I said one of my favorites, speaking aloud.

"God, grant me the serenity to accept the things I cannot change, the courage to change the things I can, and the wisdom to know the difference."

The Serenity Prayer. It had always resonated for me, and it had helped guide me through challenging moments in my life. However, until this very moment, I had never analyzed the words. It's a fairly simple prayer, and that's probably why I'd always liked it so much, but now I saw that the words have a powerful meaning. I've accepted too many things in my life when I should have had the courage to change them. I was wise enough to know the difference, but not courageous enough to change anything. Now, I'm left with regrets.

At the end of my shadow, I noticed a rustling in the wheat that wasn't due to the light breeze moving the grass.

"Who's there?" I hunched over and slowly stepped in the direction of the rustling.

Slowly, a figure began to rise out of the grass. I turned the opposite way and started running. I could hear footsteps behind me, approaching rapidly.

"Stop, stop! I'm not going to hurt you!"

I looked over my shoulder to see the man had stopped chasing me. I slowed to a stop and turned around.

"What do you want from me?" I yelled back. We were about fifty feet apart.

"I bet I can help you, but you'll need to hear me out," the man said, starting toward me with his one hand held forward. He looked as though he wanted to shake my hand.

As he got closer, my heart began to pound. I wanted to run, but I was frozen. He reached his hand out to me, and I took hold of it with my hand. That felt good.

He smiled at me and let go of my hand. "I didn't mean to startle you," he said, "but it's hard not to in a situation like this."

"Situation? What do you mean?"

"You know, your situation. Arriving here and not knowing anything about this place or what to do." He was spot on.

"Do you know me?" I wondered if he had any knowledge of why I had arrived here.

"Listen, I can help you answer some questions and provide some direction, but you'll have to trust me."

"Do I really have a choice!" It was a rhetorical question.

"I heard you saying *The Serenity Prayer*. I, too, have always liked that one. I'm not sure if I'm the answer to your prayer, but look around. Do you see any other options?"

He was right. I didn't have any other options, yet I would have to proceed cautiously.

"Who are you?" I asked him.

"Well, my name is Montgomery, but call me Monty. What's your name?"

"I'm Maggie. What?"—I motioned to his bare feet—"They don't give out shoes around here?"

Monty responded by wiggling his toes. He looked to be in his early fifties. He was very tan, to the point that his skin appeared damaged from too much sun. When we shook hands, I felt his calluses scrape along my palm. Those were definitely "working hands." His hair was dark with gray streaks doing their best to take over. He stood a stout five-seven. He was wearing jeans, a short-sleeved flannel shirt, and he was barefoot.

"If we have the pleasure of knowing each other long enough, I'll tell you that story." He laughed and walked past me raising his arm to motion for me to follow.

I shuffled right along behind him, like an obedient puppy, but I did ask him, "Where are we going?"

Monty turned around. "Let's just get this straight right now: you can't ask me that every thirty steps, OK? Just follow me, and I'll get you to where you need to go. This isn't my first time doing this, you know." There was that smile again, which made me feel at ease.

Just like that, we were off. I'd follow and try to keep my mouth shut while Monty led the way. I didn't ask him more questions—well, at least not right away.

9

We marched along for over an hour, heading west into the setting sun. The terrain didn't change much along the way. The walk was quite boring, both visually and conversationally. Monty didn't say a word after he scolded me for asking too many questions, and I kept quiet, too. Finally, I could see a slight rise coming up in the terrain. We would be on an incline soon, and, even though it was a small hill, I was hoping something promising would reveal itself when we reached the top.

"Just another hundred yards to the top of the hill," Monty said, speaking as if I were familiar with this route we were taking.

"Then what?" My patience was starting to wear thin. I wanted to know, even though I knew I was in no position to complain.

"Come over here, and I'll show you." Monty made his way over to a small patch of dirt about five feet in diameter. He sat down on a small boulder to one side, his knees right up against his chest as he started to draw in the dirt with a stick.

"This is where you are now." Monty placed a pebble in the dirt. "And this is where you entered." He placed another pebble a few inches away from the first to indicate where he'd found me.

"Now pay attention because I'm not always going to be around to hold your hand." For a brief moment he shifted his focus from the dirt to my face, and then he got up from his rock.

He took the stick and dragged it completely around the five foot circle we were sitting beside—starting to the west, proceeding north, and going east, south and back to the west until he had closed the circle right where he'd begun it.

"This is your world now," he said, his voice becoming serious. "You'll have to explore this world in each direction to figure out why the hell you are here. The only thing I can tell you with one hundred percent certainty is that it won't be easy." He paused to let those words sink in.

"Think of this circle as a clock. Right now, we're heading west which is nine o'clock. North is twelve o'clock, east is three o'clock and…" Monty stopped and looked at me, apparently making sure I was taking this in.

"And south is six o'clock," I said, finishing his sentence for him. "I get it, so why are we going west?"

"Let me finish." Monty said. "Or I can walk away right now, and you'll be free to fend for yourself." The words were strong enough on their own, but then Monty took a step toward me, pointing the stick at

10

my face.

I stepped out of the circle and looked more carefully at Monty's drawing in the dirt. The large circle had a cross in the middle, apparently indicating where I needed to go on this journey. Four stops, all equidistant from the center, with the westernmost stop just over this hill.

Monty was now looking at me like a disappointed parent with a disobedient child. He said, "Before we go any farther, you'll need to understand and respect what this is all about. I don't feel like you're willing to do that."

I've never been a patient person, and I've been accused of having a short fuse on many occasions. This situation proved to be no different.

"Stop with the bullshit, Monty. You don't know what I've been through!" I was almost yelling, and I grabbed the stick out of his hand. "If you don't want to help me, then don't. I didn't even ask for you to help me. You just showed up and volunteered. I don't even know where I am or why I'm here. How do you expect me to act?"

Monty was flustered. "OK, I'll go. Good luck to you." He turned to the east and began walking back the way we had come. "Someone else will need my help soon enough," he added, and he motioned to the sky where two vultures were circling above the same spot where the two of us had met earlier in the day. Monty picked up his pace then.

As Monty got farther and farther away, I realized I wasn't going to be able to do this all alone. I started to run toward him. "Monty!" He didn't acknowledge me.

I caught up to him and grabbed him by the left arm swiveling him around to look at me.

"Please don't do this! You're all I have." My only choice was to put my trust in Monty and let him take the lead. I was ready to do that now.

Monty took a deep breath and exhaled slowly. "You're not the first person to come here with a shitty attitude," he said, "thinking you know it all."

"I'm ready to listen, Monty, but I'm scared. It sounds like you do this a lot, but remember, this is all new to me. So, please be patient."

"Fair enough. Sometimes I get ahead of myself. Let's start over."

We went back to the circle Monty had drawn, sat on our small boulders, and Monty told me his story.

CHAPTER THREE

———◆◇◆———

Montgomery Charles Fisher was born in 1933 in a town just outside of Philadelphia. Wynnewood was tiny back then, and it hasn't grown a lot since; fewer than 14,000 people live there today. Monty was the second of two children born to Joseph and Katherine. His older sister by three years, Constance, lived only until she was eight, a bout with leukemia taking her away. Monty was five when Connie passed; he had almost nothing to remember his sister by other than the stories his parents shared and a few black-and-white photos tucked away in a family album.

Joseph was a construction worker and, like everyone he knew in the Great Depression, he went long periods without steady work, making life hard for him and his family. To his credit, Joe wasn't above working menial jobs to put food on the table. Whether he was sweeping the streets, hauling trash, or whatever else that day's work would offer, he made the best of it. Monty would learn well from his father, establishing a no-nonsense work ethic when he eventually started a career in construction as well.

Katherine migrated from Europe, Italy to be exact. Katherine Josephine Tortorelli arrived at Ellis Island in 1924 at age fifteen with only her older brother. Others in their extended family had made their way to Philadelphia several years before; Katherine and Anthony, age eighteen, left Italy after the death of their parents. The sister and brother boarded a small ship to America, leaving behind all that they knew. Just three years after Katherine arrived in the U.S., she met Joe, and they were married shortly thereafter.

Life was tough for the Fishers, but they had a strong familial bond that grew even stronger after Connie passed away. There were times after Connie's death that the family appeared to be breaking apart, but Joe and Katherine were determined to give Monty the childhood he deserved. They persevered and did just that. It was a simple life, but a good one until it all unraveled on the night of January 2, 1950.

Rarely did the Fishers enjoy a meal outside of their tiny apartment, but on this night, Joe decided that Katherine deserved to be served rather than to be the one doing the serving. Joe arrived home early from work that day as business had been slow due to the wintry weather and the end of the holiday season. When he shared the news that they'd be going out to dinner as a family, he received the responses he had expected. Katherine told him that she had already prepped a meal and why should they spend the money? Monty was thrilled, not because he didn't enjoy his mother's cooking, but because going out to eat was so rare for the family and he knew they would be going to his favorite spot, Cochran's. It had been more than a year since they had enjoyed a meal at Cochran's and at least six months since they had been out to eat anywhere. Such occasions were unique and special. The spur-of-the-moment nature of this dinner out was unusual for Joe, but Monty wasn't about to question it.

Cochran's was just four blocks away from the Fishers' apartment. Steak was the restaurant's specialty, and though the family hadn't been there recently, they each knew exactly what they'd order even before they sat down. The menu doesn't change at Cochran's; as there's no need to mess with near perfection. Fresh bread, soup, salad, and (of course) steak, plus cheesecake for dessert. A perfect evening for Joe, Katherine, and Monty. The parents caught up on everything Monty had going on in his life. Katherine, especially, enjoyed this opportunity to talk in the time she would spend prepping, cooking, and cleaning up after their usual dinners. Being able to sit across from Monty with Joe beside her meant everything to Katherine. She couldn't have asked for a better evening with the two loves of her life.

After dessert, Joe paid the bill, and the three Fishers made their way out the front door for their four-block stroll home. About halfway home, Joe sensed an odd presence just a few feet behind him. The group picked up their pace only to feel and hear the steps behind them also speed up. Joe was walking in the middle of Monty and Katherine. Katherine was holding his left hand and Monty was on his right.

Joe turned his head slightly to glance behind him and saw two men continuing their pursuit. He released his hand from Katherine and yelled for her and Monty to run. Joe then turned around, heading straight into the danger behind them. Monty listened to his father, while Katherine did not. She was about ten feet behind her husband.

It all happened in an instant. What was meant to be a robbery turned into a double homicide. Joe startled the two men by bearing down on them, prompting one of the men to fire instantly. Katherine rushed to Joe's aid and got the second bullet. Monty heard the shots and turned around to see both of his parents lying lifeless on the sidewalk. The men fired in Monty's direction and began to pursue him, but the young man ran around the corner and into an alley, seeking cover in a dumpster. He listened from his hiding spot as the assailants looked around for him and then ran away. Someone had called the police, and their arrival saved Monty's life, but it was too late for his parents. In the blink of an eye Monty was all by himself.

At the age of seventeen, Monty experienced more pain than most people do in a lifetime. The tragic ending to their special night would weigh heavily on him for the rest of his life. If only he had ignored his father's directive to run! If only he had charged the robbers with his father, maybe the three of them could have survived! Monty questioned his actions that evening, and as time went on, his guilt became heavier.

High school graduation came and went. Monty's aunt and uncle had provided him with a place to stay, but not much else. On his eighteenth birthday he joined the Army, spending four years serving his country. During those four years, the fragile relationship he had with his aunt and uncle dissolved. No longer did Monty have any contact with the Fisher or Tortorelli families. He formed a couple of relationships, but then he walked away from them. He was with Janet for about a year and then Gloria for about two. All the time, Monty was careful not to get too close. He didn't want to care too much. He didn't want the pain of losing someone else he loved. He'd rather be the one to walk away than risk Janet, Gloria, or anyone else walking away first.

January 2 would once again become a significant date in the life of Montgomery Charles Fisher. Ten years had passed since his parents' murder. Monty continued to struggle with guilt and decided he had suffered long enough. His landlord would find him hanging from a beam in the small, dingy basement apartment that he was renting at the time. On the floor a note scratched down on a yellow legal pad read in pencil:

Mom and Dad,
I should have done more for you both that night and I'm sorry.
I can't do this anymore alone. All I want is to be with you both.
This may not be the most graceful way to go out, but I just
don't care anymore. I hope I find you, and we can be a family
again.
Love,
Monty

Just like that, he was gone, and sadly enough no one knew or
cared. He truly did die alone.

Both Monty and I had tears running down our faces. I rose from my spot
in the clearing and walked over to Monty. I embraced him tightly, and he
reciprocated with a bear hug of his own. We were both carrying a lot of
pain and looking for answers. Hopefully, we will be able to help each
other navigate this world and find the answers that would allow us to rest
in peace.

"I'm so sorry Monty," I said once we were eye to eye after our
embrace.

"Don't feel sorry for me. I don't deserve any pity." Monty's gaze
wandered into the distance, and then he began to walk away. His mind
was shifting back to the task at hand.

"Let's get moving," he said. "You don't want to jump into the
darkness." Monty picked up his pace, and I hurried behind.

"Jump?" Chills went down my spine.

"Yep, you heard me: jump." Monty's tone was casual. "Just stay
close to me."

We continued west with the sun blazing into our eyes. I held my
hand to my forehead, shielding my eyes from the sun's rays as the incline
became a bit steeper. I could now see that we were arriving at the edge
of what appeared to be a cliff.

"Get up here and take a look at this." Monty waved his right arm
from left to right with a satisfying grin.

The edge of the cliff rose about a hundred feet from a body of
water that was so dark a blue that it looked almost black. There were
small waves with crests in a fluorescent blue that looked electric. Across
this body of water was a field of the greenest grass I'd ever seen. It

reminded me of the grass in one of the state parks we used to visit for family picnics. The kids would roll around in the grass while Cliff and I watched them play. I remember the smell of that grass and how cozy it was to just lay in it with Cliff by my side. Surrounding the grassy area that was before me now were at least a hundred trees in bloom—a bank of yellow flowers rising about forty feet above the luscious grass. In the distance I could see a path that seemed to go for just a few feet and then abruptly ended.

"Wow, this is absolutely beautiful." I was amazed at what I was looking at. "Is that Heaven?"

Monty let out a small chuckle. "That's what you all say."

"Well, then what is this place?" I continued to take in the beauty.

"Hopefully this is where you'll get some answers to why you're here, and more importantly, a little direction on how to find your kids." Monty patted my shoulder and glanced down at the dark water below.

"How many times have you brought people here?"

"I've lost track. More than a hundred but less than a thousand." He raised his eyebrows and winked at me.

While I still had doubts as to Monty's genuineness, I was ready to do whatever he had planned for me. He never answered my question about whether this was Heaven, but if his guidance takes me to my children, that would be good enough for me. That's all I wanted.

Monty reached his right hand toward me. "It's time, Maggie. Take my hand."

"So, we're really going to jump." My left hand was shaking uncontrollably as I placed it in Monty's hand.

"Listen carefully. We'll jump with our hands locked together, but when you hit the Memory Pool, we'll get separated. I know this is easier said than done, but just go with it. Remember, you're already dead, so little things like breathing are inconsequential. You won't drown." Monty squeezed my hand a little tighter, and my heart started racing.

"Did you say 'Memory Pool?'"

"Yep, you'll see. Now let's do this!" Monty's voice rose.

"Oh, my God!" There was no turning back now.

"One, two, three!" We jumped. We went feet first, my legs kicking wildly while Monty was in a graceful freefall with barely any movement. I clutched his hand as tight as I could, knowing that we would be separated on impact. I could tell that we were falling at a rapid pace, but it felt like we were moving in slow motion. My eyes locked in on the small path in the distance, and for a brief moment I saw three people standing side-by-side and holding hands. The sun wrapped around each of them producing long shadows. I tried to improve my view, and then we slammed into the water.

The velocity of our hundred-foot drop pushed us deep into the water. Just like Monty had warned, we were separated. He was nowhere in sight, and panic began to set in. My natural instinct had me kicking and paddling frantically in an effort to get to the surface. I quickly realized that despite my strongest efforts, I wasn't getting any closer to the top. The sunlight was shining through the water from above, mixing the dark blue with rays of a fierce orange. I stopped struggling for a moment, gazing up at this incredible sight. Suddenly, my view changed, and I had a horrific vision of the night my children and I were murdered. At first, I didn't understand what I was seeing, but after a while I realized that the aftermath of Cliff's rampage was right in front of me. Seeing my children post-massacre was gut wrenching. I screamed, trying to cover my eyes. But I couldn't. An outside force was controlling me, and I was unable to shake this vision. It was upon me, and I had no choice but to take in every gory detail. This wasn't Heaven! This Memory Pool felt like Hell!

I continued to remain underwater, neither descending nor ascending, while I was being forced to focus on the tragedy that had taken my innocent children's lives. Room by room, I was guided through my bloody and ravaged home until I reached the door to the master bedroom. I braced myself for what was sure to be a grisly scene. I wasn't in control of this tour through what had been our cozy home. I decided I was ready to enter the room, and I attempted to move forward. I couldn't. I looked down to my feet, which were now bare, and I noticed a trail of blood that appeared to be coming from the bedroom. A body had been dragged through the doorway. Once again, I made an attempt to push myself forward—and once again I failed. The door directly in front of me was closed.

Then I noticed that what I was seeing wasn't the actual door to the master bedroom. Everything else I had seen as I was moved throughout the house was the same as when I had left it. Only this door was different. All of our bedroom doors were white, solid wood with six panels and beautiful antique doorknobs. I had found these knobs at an antique store just outside of Cleveland. I remember seeing them and knowing they'd be perfect for our house. The only problem was that they'd been short one knob. The antique store had a showroom in the front and what amounted to a warehouse in the back. The owner of the store gave us the green light to search through the warehouse and, to my surprise, Cliff and I had located one more knob. We were thrilled with our find. We felt like the guys from American Pickers securing a big score.

Cliff and I had been in such a good place back then. I wished I could go back to that time and do it all over again. Of course, that's easier said than done. What could I actually have done differently? There's no way to pinpoint the one problem that caused our marriage to fall off the track. It's never just one thing, one big thing. It's a bunch of small things. Those tiny things are the most important sign of a healthy marriage. Get the small things right, and the big ones will take care of themselves.

The door I was being forced to stare at was cheap. It was hollow faux wood with an imitation brass knob that was barely attached to the door. I felt a warming sensation under my feet. I looked down to see a pool of blood beginning to develop around me. I felt paralyzed from the neck down as the blood began to fill the area I was standing in. My feet disappeared in this blood as it continued to rise. Inch by inch, the blood started to engulf my entire body. The door began to open, slowly. The blood was up to my chest and moving quickly. A bloody hand appeared from behind the opening door. Then, to my horror, I could see the rest of the body, covered in blood from head to toe. I wasn't surprised. I was looking at my post-murder self. No expression, just a lifeless stare greeted me at my bedroom doorway. The blood moved from my murdered body to me. I closed my mouth tightly, but I had no way to pinch my nose and my eyes were wide open, incapable of being shut.

Everything turned red when the blood reached my eyes. Then a massive push came from below my feet, driving me toward the surface of the Memory Pool. I looked up to see the familiar bright orange and electric blue above me as I quickly ascended. My head broke through the surface of the water, and I regained control of my body. I bobbed up and down for a bit, still confused and mentally bruised from what I had seen underwater. I could see the shore only a couple hundred feet away, and I propelled myself forward by kicking my legs. I glanced over my shoulder and looked up to the top of the cliff. It seemed much higher than the hundred feet Monty had said it was.

The pool was now shallow enough for me to touch the bottom, and I began walking to the shore. My dress had a tear or two in it, but otherwise it looked exactly like it had before I made the jump. It wasn't bloodstained. In front of me, the vivid green grass covered the area between the pool and the trees with the yellow flowers. Normally, a view as stunning as this would be worth enjoying for a bit, but this wasn't a sight-seeing tour. Monty had pointed me in the right direction, and it was time for me to venture into the unknown solo.

A sliver of the sun still remained on the horizon. The thought of navigating the unknown in the dark scared the bejesus out of me. I turned around to take another look back to where I had come from with the hope of spotting Monty. The Memory Pool was so calm that it looked like a sheet of glass. It was gorgeous. It was difficult to comprehend all the terror I'd experienced under that smooth body of water. Monty referred to it as a pool, but it was a reasonably sized lake, probably about twenty acres. He was nowhere in sight, and I felt lost.

I focused on the Memory Pool. As I panned back and forth a small ripple in the center of the water caught my eye. The sun had disappeared now, making way for the moon. The moon was only about two days away from being completely full. The brightness of the moonlight reflected off of the Memory Pool, shedding more light on the ripple in the center—which was no longer just a ripple. The water began to get extremely rough, and it appeared that the disturbance was coming from under the water's surface as there was no wind to create the effect I was seeing. Suddenly, a body was launched from underneath the water rising about five feet above the surface. The person was flailing and crying out. I made a move to run to help this person, but I was held back. A vine had wrapped itself around both of my legs and was holding me in place. I fell forward on my knees, reaching back to my ankles and calves trying to pry myself loose.

"Swim to me!" I yelled while I continued to battle with the vines.

The figure in the water began to gain composure and slowly swam toward the shore.

"Who's there?" he called out. It sounded like a teenage boy. My heart raced as the voice sounded just like Christopher's.

I frantically grabbed at the vines, successfully freeing myself just as the boy reached the shore. I sprinted toward him.

"Christopher?" I was about fifty feet away. The darkness and the slight glare of moonlight off of what was once again a calm Memory Pool did not give me a clear view.

"Stop right there," the boy yelled, raising his arms up.

I stopped, and suddenly I could see him. This was not my son.

"Stay away from me," the boy said, shuffling to one side, ready to dash past me.

"Calm down," I said, trying to ease his fears. "I won't hurt you."

"Yeah, I've heard that before. Now step aside and let me pass." He pointed over my head in the direction where I'd seen the three figures holding hands during my jump.

The boy looked to be about fifteen. He was Hispanic, with shoulder-length black hair. His hair lay neatly in pin straight strands across his shoulders and back. Of course, the tank top he was wearing was soaked as were his navy blue dress pants. He, too, had no shoes.

"So, you've been here before." I reached down to rub my left leg. The vines had interfered with the circulation and had left a numbing sensation.

"Who sent you to find me?" the boy asked.

"Sent me?"

"Yes. Just leave me alone, all of you." He glanced back over his shoulder as if he thought someone were following him.

"All of who? I am not with anyone, I promise." I took a couple of steps forward.

"Prove it." He backed up the same two steps, re-establishing the space between us.

"I don't know how to prove it." What could I say? "I just got here myself. Monty jumped off of the cliff with me, but I haven't seen him since. Do you know Monty?"

The boy's expression changed from fear to acceptance. Monty must have been the magic word.

"Fuck, Monty," he said. I was surprised when that prompted a level of discomfort to run through me.

"What do you know about Monty?" He was the only other person that I'd seen here.

"He's a fucking liar, and he's stuck out there with the vultures for good reason." The boy pointed to the direction where I had entered.

"Please help me understand," I told him. "I promise you that no one sent me here for you."

20

"OK, I'll give you a chance. But you'll only get one. I've been here too long, and I have no patience for shit like this. If you lie, you're fucked. And, believe me, I'll make getting hit with a hammer fifty-three times feel like a day at the park." With that, a rush of heat pierced my body, and I fainted.

I hit the ground, with the right side of my face taking the brunt of this collapse. I felt a hand grab me on my left shoulder and flip me over so I was facing up. My vision started to come back. I heard the boy say, "Hey, snap out of it!" and I felt a light slap on each check.

As I regained consciousness, the fear that had caused me to faint came right back, and I grabbed the boy's wrist, causing him to seize my arm with his free hand.

"Let go now, bitch!" He squeezed my arm and drove in his fingernails until I was bleeding.

I released his arm, and he pulled me up by my wrist with one hand and my hair with the other.

"Stop it, please!" I was on my knees, pleading with him to let me go. He let go of my wrist and shoved my head down to the sandy ground again.

"Tell PopCon that I'm on to them, and don't let me see you again." He stepped over me toward the grassy area, his stride breaking into a sprint.

I turned my head in his direction and watched him disappear along the path that led to the break in the trees. He moved quickly. Tears began rolling down my face, washing away the remaining bits of sand on my cheek. It had all been a blur since my arrival, leaving me with no time to grieve for my children or myself. Now, sitting on the magnificent shore of the Memory Pool, I felt it all come crashing down on me. I broke down. Death was not supposed to be like this. Everything I had been taught seemed like a sham. I was taught that if I led a good life—caring for others, respecting others—that I'd be rewarded with a place by God's side in Heaven. I knew that my life hadn't been perfect, but what had I done to deserve this? My purpose in this new realm was undefined. I couldn't allow this to be the end for me. I had always believed that there is a Heaven, but this brief experience has confirmed there is also a Hell. What worried me most was that this might be Hell. It felt like Hell.

I gathered my composure and stood up from the sand. The

moonlight was shining on the Memory Pool, and the light provided me with a fairly clear view of my surroundings. I noticed that I wasn't tired or hungry. I knew that both of those feelings should be taking over my body by now, but I wasn't experiencing either one of them. That seemed strange. I found myself wishing that Monty were here to answer my questions. In the short time that he'd been gone, I had completely failed at anything I tried to undertake. And here I was: sitting on the shore of the Memory Pool with more questions than I had answers.

My instinct told me to find a spot to sleep until morning, but my stubbornness said to keep moving. The only route that seemed to make sense was going straight ahead through the trees, the same direction the boy had taken. However, I didn't want to ever run into him again. Somehow, he thought he knew who I was and thought I was sent for him. What did he mean by PopCon? Perhaps Monty was PopCon?

I looked down to my wrist, the same wrist the boy had ground his nails into. To my surprise, there were no marks. I could remember the pain of his grip. I had seen the blood with my own eyes, yet now there wasn't one mark—not so much as a scratch. So, I wasn't tired or hungry, and my wounds healed immediately. This made me wonder if what I'm experiencing is real. Maybe it's just an illusion of some sort. The emotional weight I'd been experiencing was almost unbearable; I felt weighed down by it. It occurred to me that I'd been learning about this place as an exercise of intellect. It could be that my mind is the most powerful tool I have. If so, I'd need to channel my energy to my brain. Every time I'd lost confidence—and that's easy to do in this mental world—I'd gone into a negative downward spiral. I could see that right now, I needed to find something positive about this situation, something I could use to push myself forward. My mission was to reunite with my children. That's all that mattered to me. If I came across that boy again, I'd just have to convince him that I'm not anyone to be scared off. This situation was, truly, what I made of it, and I could make it work. I needed to do that for my kids and for my own eternal peace. Rest in peace, that's what they say, and that's what I hoped to find—one way or another.

I directed myself toward that mysterious spot through the trees and confidently marched ahead. The grass beneath my feet was cold and, as I moved forward, it began to get colder. The moon shone onto the yellow flowering trees on either side of me. The grassy space narrowed as I approached my destination. The grass came to an end, giving way to a dirt path that was about ten feet wide. I arrived at a break in the grass where it met the path and I came to a stop.

I don't know why I felt compelled to pause before stepping onto the dirt, but I did, taking that moment to look again at my surroundings. To my amazement, it appeared as though the Memory Pool had frozen over. I focused in closer, and in the middle of the pool, I could see an arm rising out of the ice. The sight of this arm—just below the elbow—coming up from the frozen surface startled me, and I stumbled backward onto the dirt path. In that instant, the Memory Pool thawed and the arm came back to life, beginning a frantic flailing. This was the second time I'd witnessed this phenomenon—and the third, if I counted my own experience. Perhaps it was my naivete or my faith in humanity, but my instinct was to rush down to the shore of the Memory Pool to help this person. Both of my feet were now squarely on the dirt path. I took a step in the direction of the Memory Pool, and immediately the pool iced over again, leaving the individual that was in it helpless. Now her head was visible along with the same arm that had previously risen above the frozen surface.

"Get back!" A woman behind me shrieked.

I turned back around, returning my feet to the dirt path. I could hear that behind me the Memory Pool had once again thawed. There was a splashing sound as the individual in the pool struggled to find her composure, just as I had done previously.

"You can't go back there now," this new woman told me. "See what happens when you do? Give her a chance, just as I gave you." The woman watched as the person in the pool reached the shallow waters.

I was annoyed. "I didn't know!" I said. "How was I supposed to know?" There was an edge in my voice that hadn't been there during my earlier confrontation with the boy. My abruptness startled the woman, and she responded with a similar edge. I couldn't tell whether she was scared or angry.

"You can't ever go back," she said. "If you do, you'll ruin it for those who follow you." She reached out and lightly touched my shoulder with her wrinkled hand, and her chin dropped to her chest. She appeared to be praying.

In a moment, her head rose, and she looked straight at me with the most stunning hazel eyes I had ever seen. Her eyes were young, not at all like the rest of her. It seemed that a young woman had been trapped

23

in an aged body. Her hair was long, almost down to her waist. Even though it was gray, it was gorgeous and with a slight curl to it. She stood about five-seven. She was slim. And she was barefoot—a common theme. The dress she was wearing was tattered, but clearly had once been an elegant gown, possibly from the late eighteen hundreds or early nineteen hundreds.

"My name is Joanna," she said. "What's yours?"

"Maggie. My name is Maggie." I saw that letting my guard down was going to be difficult.

"I understand your anxiety, Maggie. It's OK to be nervous. I was too when I first arrived."

Joanna's hand continued to rest on my shoulder, and I tried to be gentle in taking it off. "I have to go now," I told her. "Please don't get in my way." I started walking down the path.

Joanna kept pace, walking beside me. "Don't you want to know where you're headed?" she asked. "I've been there already."

I stopped and turned toward Joanna, looking deep into those hazel eyes. There was a trustworthy vibe that I could sense deep down. It may have been her appearance that put me at ease. She reminded me of a harmless grandmother, someone who posed no threat to me. I let her continue alongside me as she revealed what she knew about this place.

"I've stopped counting the days I've been here," she said, echoing Monty's sentiment. "Days and time really don't matter."

Joanna didn't walk like an old lady. Her brisk strides were difficult to keep up with. It was clear that she had walked this path back and forth for a long time. I began to notice that she was placing her feet in specific spots on the path as we marched forward. She did this without looking down at her feet. It was instinct for her now, and that was a bit maddening to see. Joanna was trapped here, which made my fear grow for the potential hopelessness that I might face.

"Where will this path lead us?" I asked, still mesmerized by Joanna's ability to step perfectly into her previous footprints.

"Perhaps it would be best if we sat down for a bit. Your question is a typical one, and I know how these conversations go. Yeah, let's have a seat." Joanna stepped off the path to our right. Once again, she stayed inside her previous footprints, which led us down a short hillside, giving way to a clearing with a couple of logs.

Joanna sat on the log facing the path, and I settled down on the other.

"This path has been traveled by millions of souls," she said. "It's the pathway to Heaven," I was happy just hearing the word "heaven."

"Do you know if my children walked this path?" I rose to my feet in anticipation.

"Yes, I saw your children, but not along this path." I tried to interrupt, but Joanna proceeded with more information. "That's a good thing. It means they're in Heaven."

Hearing this, my eyes began to tear up. "They are? How can you be sure?" I stayed on my feet and began pacing and rubbing my hands together, nervously.

"I saw them at the pass. They are looking for you, but you'll have to do the finding. They can't."

"They can't help me? Why not?"

Joanna looked at me with disappointment. I had touched on a sensitive issue.

"Maggie, the Path of Lost Souls is full of people who have never been able to help themselves. That's why we're stuck here—all of us, including me." Joanna's eyes watered up, but she refrained from shedding any tears.

"The Path of Lost Souls? Why is it called that?"

"As I said, millions go down this path, but millions don't pass through. Some find their way back through the Memory Pool, but most are trapped here for eternity." Joanna placed both of her palms on her chest.

"If there are millions of people trapped here, why don't I see anyone else?" I looked around. It was just the two of us here.

"We appear when we want to appear, and we get involved when we feel we can help. That's why I'm here for you. But if you can't help yourself, you'll end up just like me and the others. I can't do all of the work for you. It's not allowed." Joanna seemed to have a blueprint of the process.

The two of us sat on the logs adjacent to The Path of Lost Souls, deep in conversation until the sun came up. Joanna seemed to share everything she knew about this place. My observation about her dress was accurate. It was from the late eighteen hundreds—1897 to be exact. Her apparent age wasn't indicative of her life. She had never made it past thirty-seven. She told me that in this place, I shouldn't trust anyone's appearance, citing herself as a perfect example. Joanna looked like a woman in her late eighties or early nineties, but her life had ended well before that point. Her young-looking eyes and brisk pace made sense now. She was a young woman trapped in an old woman's body. I thought back to my confrontation with the boy and his mature way of communicating—more to the point, his vulgar way of demeaning me. A young boy wouldn't speak like that! I began to wonder what I looked like.

"How old do I look?" I asked,

Joanna smiled. "Come over here and we can take a look." She led me deeper into the wooded area and we came to a small pond. "See for yourself."

I approached the water slowly, not knowing what to expect. I wondered if my face looked like it had when I saw the image of my bloody self in the Memory Pool. When I got to the edge of the pond, I leaned forward. The reflection staring at me was my sixteen-year-old self. The dress I was wearing was straight out of the eighties, and I vividly remember where I wore it for the first and only time. It was my friend Diana's sweet sixteen party. I had hated this dress. One of the boys, Mark Benson, embarrassed me when he made a stupid joke about it. I don't remember what the joke was, but everyone heard it, and everyone laughed at me. I was devastated. I called my mom right away and asked her to pick me up. Of course, I took it out on her because of my ugly dress. We didn't have a lot of money when I was growing up. My dad had disappeared, leaving Mom to function as the sole provider for me and my younger brother. By "disappear" I mean he left us. He left us without a word or a note. I was ten, and my brother was only six. Martin barely remembers Dad, but I do. It was best that he left.

About four months after my humiliating experience at Diana's birthday party, I would meet Cliff in the hallway of our high school. That's when the two of us began hanging out together. I'm starting to understand how things work here. It makes me wonder how the afterlife will be for him. I know that he deserves to be punished, perhaps even going to Hell for what he did. I've tried to hate Cliff, but for some reason, I'm unable to hate him. I don't know why, but that feeling has not consumed me. I don't want to be filled with hate anyway.

"Joanna, do you mind if I ask how you died?" I continued to

stare at my reflection enjoying the innocence in the face staring back at me.

"No, not at all. What I had really didn't have a name back then. They simply labeled me as insane, deranged or whatever the diagnosis was that particular week." A slight smile revealed itself as Joanna stood beside me reviewing her own reflection.

My sixteen-year-old reflection side-by-side with Joanna's thirty-seven-year-old reflection reminded me of the special moments I had with my mother. We would often sit at our kitchen table, each of us with a cup of hot tea, talking together into the night. The bond we shared was beyond the typical mother-daughter relationship. She was my best friend.

"I used to have conversations with my mom like this. Sometimes, we'd stay up all night, but never regretted it the next day, no matter how tired I was." A small ripple moved through the pond and then settled again.

"Hopefully, you'll find her, too," Joanna said, and then, much to my disappointment, she stepped away from the pond.

I followed along as we made our way back to the path. I'd enjoyed our time at the pond, but I knew it was time to move on. The idea of being able to find my mother in addition to my children was exciting. I was ready to take the next step on this unpredictable journey.

We arrived at the edge of the path, and I asked, "So, now what?" Joanna had turned us westward.

She said, "You need to help yourself now. This isn't about me, and I'm afraid my tagging along will only hinder your progress. This is where I let you go, Maggie." Joanna positioned herself in front of me with the path to her back.

The reality of wandering off alone began to set in. "I don't feel like I'm ready for this," I said.

"You're as ready as you'll ever be," she told me. "Please don't take this the wrong way, but I hope I never see you again. If I don't, that means you've made it. Knowing that you're at peace would bring some semblance of peace to my soul as well. And that's what I'm looking for. Other than simply helping others, that's a reason I do this: I'm trying to rest in peace, too." Joanna stepped aside then, clearing the way for me to leave.

"Thank you, Joanna. I can't thank you enough." I took hold of her hands before letting go and giving way to a hug. A quick hug. I knew I had to go on alone.

CHAPTER FOUR

I hoped Joanna was right. I hoped I would never see her again. Maybe if I make it to Heaven, I'll be able to return the favor and help her find peace. Her predicament scared me, at least in part because it really didn't make much sense. From what she'd said, I couldn't figure out why she was stuck there. There may be no consistent characteristics or backgrounds among those who were stuck along the Path of Lost Souls, but Joanna didn't seem like she should be there. I've always believed that each person has their own purpose in life, and perhaps this translates to the afterlife as well. Joanna had helped me, and I feel that she must have helped others as well. I hoped the more help she gave people, the closer she would get to Heaven.

For a while the path had been fairly straight, but now it was beginning to wind back and forth. As I've come to find, the scenery here is gorgeous. Trees with deep green leaves thickly lined the path. The only noise I'd heard had come from my own feet walking along the dirt path, one step after another. Then, in the distance I saw a break in the trees on one side of the path. A huge boulder stood about twenty-five feet tall and ten to fifteen feet wide at the base. This rock—like a monolith— almost came to a point at its top. As I got closer to it, I could see that the path wound around the boulder, making a ninety degree turn to the right. I stopped in the middle of the path, rotating around to get a better view of everything around me—and even above me. I had been walking in shade for most of this time—the sunshine had barely broken through the dense trees—but that was about to change.

The brightness wrapped around the boulder and shone out onto the path, seemingly inviting me to step forward. I didn't resist it. With a few more steps, I arrived next to the boulder. The rock had an odd-looking surface. A film of what appeared to be algae covered most of it.

I reached out with one hand and found it slippery to the touch. There was moisture condensed on it; the rock was dripping with water. To the left of the boulder, a clear line appeared on the path; the shaded area was sharply distinguished from the bright area. It reminded me of my arrival on the path, the point where the grass had met the dirt. When I'd tried to turn around there, my steps in the wrong direction had caused the Memory Pool to freeze over. That was when Joanna proclaimed that I could never go back. Now, I was apparently standing at another crossroad. I wondered if my next step forward would alter my surroundings and cause pain to me or someone else. My journey was about to change again; I was sure of it.

I placed my right foot on the bright side of the path and followed immediately with my left foot. The brightness blinded me, and I felt myself being pushed forward. I had no control. I felt pressure in my lower back as my toes scraped alternately along the ground. I turned my head from side to side, frantically trying to get a glimpse of what was pushing me from behind. I couldn't see anything. I began to rise a bit from the ground and, still blind from the bright light, I had no idea what was causing my unexpected trajectory. Then, the pressure on my lower back subsided, and my vision began to return. I found myself levitating approximately four feet above the path. I noticed that my heart rate was at a surprisingly normal level, and I hovered there, waiting for whatever would come next.

The scenery had changed drastically. No longer was I in shade and covered by the lush greenery. Twenty feet ahead, the path came to an abrupt end. The path stopped at a translucent wall, which stretched to both the right and the left as far as I could see. I looked up and found no end in that direction either. I still hovered in place. I seemed to have full movement in my body, but I could not get any closer to the wall. At first, the wall appeared to be solid, but then I noticed a slight movement in it, a ripple that seemed to flow throughout the wall. Perhaps this wall was penetrable.

And, as it turned out, it was. First, I could see a figure approaching from behind the wall on ground level. I was still hovering above in my same position twenty feet away. I began kicking my legs with the goal of getting closer. I felt that I had to reach the wall and break through it. Then there was a bulge in the wall, a mass that appeared about three feet off the ground. Something or someone was trying to push through. This began to take recognizable form when I saw a hand emerging from the wall. This hand was covered in the substance that made up the wall, and soon the rest of the arm followed the hand. The outline of the person's face became visible as well, and, clearly, a figure was trying to push past through the wall to get to my side.

It came, first finger by finger, then the whole hand, and then—stretching a bit—the arm and shoulder. Finally, there was a face that had pushed through the wall and revealed itself.

My heart sank, and I kicked as hard as I could to break free from my spot. The face was Reese's. It was my sweet little baby girl, poking through this wall and locking her bright, blue eyes on mine.

"Mommy!" Reese yelled—but with joy, not fear.

"Oh, my baby." I began to sob uncontrollably. Reese appeared happy and at peace. According to Joanna, my children had made it to Heaven and this sighting seemed to confirm that notion.

"Come over here," Reese called to me. "We want you to be with us. Why are you there?" My daughter had asked the question that I had been asking myself from the moment I arrived. What was I doing here? Then I had a question for Reese.

"You said 'we.' Are your brothers with you?"

"Yes, Mommy, they're here, too." Reese smiled, and I felt a sense of relief.

No matter what else happened now, at least I knew my children had made it to Heaven. As I looked at my beautiful little daughter, my moment of elation began to turn into a sense of guilt. I had done this. I hadn't swung the hammer, but I had driven Cliff to it. I was equally to blame. As I hovered there, taking in this remorse, a frightening thought went through my mind. I might be going to Hell. This might be my one chance to say goodbye to my children before going on to the fate I deserved. When Cliff and I had gotten married, we thought we'd be together forever. It seemed likely that we would be together for eternity—but rather than Heaven, we'd be together in Hell.

The pressure in my lower back returned as the invisible force lowered me to just inches from the ground. Then the pressure increased, and I was pushed forward again. I moved only twenty feet, but it seemed to take forever. I finally arrived at the wall, just inches away from Reese. I wanted to give her a big hug and a kiss. I reached forward, and so did she. Our hands touched, and then my dream moment turned into a

31

nightmare.

Reese had been revealed to me in such a beautiful way—and then she was withdrawn from me, horrifically. Her beautiful little hand turned to bone, one finger at a time. Her soft skin vanished under my fingers, and I was left holding the skeletal remains of what had been her hand. This transformation continued up her arm to her shoulder eventually overtaking her head and face. I was now face-to-face with the skeletal remains of my sweet daughter. I held on tightly to her fingers, hoping this would reverse the transformation. It didn't, and after a minute or two I was soon pulled away and so was Reese.

Then Reese was gone, back behind the wall, I was left once again with more questions than answers. My body dropped to the ground, the brightness subsided, and the wall became solid. I rolled over onto my stomach, and for a moment I pounded the ground beneath me. Finally, I jumped up and, running over to the wall, I began pounding the wall with my fist. Nothing happened. I was not being allowed to pass through or to see my children. Blood rolled down the side of my fist onto my wrist then my forearm. I fell to my knees in defeat, hanging my head and crying. The pain running through my body was greater than any pain I had ever felt. The last time I felt anything close to this was when my mom passed away, but this is much harder for me.

I had figured out that sleeping doesn't exist in the afterlife, now I saw that even though a body doesn't shut down, a mind does. After this experience with Reese, my mind shut down. I sat immovable right next to the wall where I had touched Reese's hand. I have no idea how much time passed. When I'd snapped out of my daze, it was dark again. I was now left to backtrack down the path on my own.

I wanted Joanna to help me figure out what to do next. I refused to believe that I was destined to be lost among the other lost souls on this path. I just couldn't let that happen. Broken-hearted though I was, I wasn't going to give up. Joanna had been quite clear that my fate would be determined by how I reacted, responded, and thought. And I knew that I was going to see my children again.

The blood that had dried on my fists and forearms began to flake off. I examined my hands closer but could find no evidence of scratches or wounds. The only physical proof of my frenzy was the dried blood on my forearms. There was just blood—no cuts, scrapes, or bruises. My mind was bruised, though. The emotions I'd felt seeing Reese—and losing her again—were paralyzing me with fear and uncertainty. Deep down I knew I wouldn't pass through the wall, but still I thought I might have an outside hope of getting through.

The very thought of backtracking down the path made me cold with fury. They call it the path of lost souls, but I think it's the path of losers. Losers who'd led poor lives and would be stuck there for eternity. I didn't want to be associated with these people. Even Joanna. Just look at her. She was content to be a shepherd along the path, giving her two cents to anyone who came along, thinking that she actually had a hand in getting anyone into Heaven. She had done nothing for me besides point me down a path I would have ventured on with or without her advice.

I didn't move from the wall. I continued to sit there, feeling sorry for myself and deepening my anger toward Joanna.

Finally, I took a deep breath and tried to regain some composure. I lifted my head and looked back down the path to where the boulder rose up out of the ground. The moon had once again risen and was shining as brightly as it had shortly after my arrival. I saw that I had a choice: I could stay here and hope for another chance to pass through the wall or I could pick myself up and return to the Memory Pool. I chose the latter.

I tore off a small piece of my dress and set it at the base of the wall. I wanted to leave something for Reese to find if she came back looking for me. This ratty old dress was all that I had to give right now. I hoped she'd be able to retrieve it. I knew that we might not see each other again.

I felt defeated as I trudged along the path, turning the corner by the boulder and making my way through the winding portion of the path. Everything looked familiar, which I took as a good sign. There were moments when I felt like I was becoming an expert at navigating this world. Then reality would set in, and I knew the only expectation I should have was to have no expectations. The thing was, every step I took could lead me to salvation or to another setback.

I arrived at the spot in the woods where Joanna and I'd spent time conversing and enjoying our reflections. She was nowhere to be seen, and I decided to stand beside the pond again. I had loved looking at my reflection; it took me back to a time in life when my worries were minimal. My biggest issues then revolved around my little circle of friends. Of course, I saw those problems as overwhelming and insurmountable, but they were just a small bump in the road. Just part of growing up. I had even looked forward to Reese becoming a teenager. A lot of parents despise the behavior of their teenage children, but something about Reese gave me confidence that she was going to be different. Maybe that's why I was stuck at this pond, staring at the sixteen-year-old me! See, Reese and I looked exactly alike. Every step of the way, from infancy to nine years old, she was a carbon copy of her mom. Now, I'd never get to see her go to a sweet sixteen party, graduate from high school, go to college, get married, or have kids. Those moments have been taken away from us.

All I had right now was my reflection in this pond. There wasn't much to smile about right now, but I can't help but smile—knowing as I knew that the face looking back at me from the pond might as well be Reese's happy face. She'd never be a sixteen-year-old, worrying about which dress to wear to her friend's party, but at least I could see her smile back at me for this brief moment. I loved that kid.

CHAPTER FIVE

A rustling in the leaves off the path behind me broke up my special moment with Reese. I turned to find my old friend, Joanna.

"I was afraid it might be you," Joanna said. "I'm sorry, dear." She shuffled through the leaves until she was standing in front of me.

"What can I do now?" I wasn't ready to accept that my fate was to be another soul lost along this path—just like Joanna herself.

"I was praying that you'd make it." She took my hand, and when she noticed the blood on my wrist and forearm, her mouth dropped open.

"This is a good sign," she said, holding up my wrist. "A very good sign!"

"What do you mean?" I was confused as to why blood on my forearm did anything to improve my situation.

"This is rare." Joanna was smiling now. "I've only seen it a handful of times, and each time those souls removed themselves from here."

"Tell me what to do, please." My excitement began to build: I might get another chance!

"Yes, there is a way to get out of here, but you'll be faced with a moral conundrum." Joanna walked over to the path, stopping when she stood in its middle, facing east. She said that six times before she had witnessed others returning from the wall with blood somewhere on their bodies. It seems that this blood, which was from a wound of some sort, was not the person's own blood. It was from behind the wall.

I held both up my arms, letting Joanna take a closer look at the dried blood.

"See," she said, "this line of blood runs exactly along your vein in this arm. Now, let me see the other arm." She looked closely at my left wrist and nodded with approval.

I hadn't noticed before, but she was right. The blood on the outside of my skin traveled the exact path of my veins. I didn't understand the significance of this, but to Joanna it meant a lot. Evidently, she had seen six other individuals with the same thing, and all six had left the path never to return.

"Let's go," Joanna said. "It's time to go back to the pool." Joanna had a hop in her step as she led me back to the Memory Pool. While we walked, she told me a bit more about my potential fate and why I'd be challenged morally if I chose to listen to her direction. "Another soul will be affected by what you choose to do," she said. She reminded me about the way the Memory Pool had frozen over every time I stepped back onto the grass.

I was horrified. "Does this mean I have to allow someone to freeze over in the pool?" The thought of being responsible for something like that horrified me.

"No," Joanna said. "It's worse than that." Joanna and I had just then arrived at the edge of the path with the Memory Pool visible in front of us.

"Worse?" I looked down at my feet as they were just off the grass.

"You see," she said. "You'll need to enter the pool with another soul. Only one of you will make it out. I don't know what will happen to the other soul, but only one will make it out." Her voice faltered as she shared this final piece of information with me.

"Wait a second," I said. "That doesn't sound right. You're saying that I may not make it out!" My enthusiasm for this venture was waning.

Joanna, usually so gracious, became adamant. "What do you want me to tell you? This is your only chance. Take it or leave it!"

Seeing Joanna get upset just escalated the intensity for me. I needed to know more. "Who is the other soul?" I asked her. "And how does this work?"

"What you're actually doing," Joanna told me, "is hijacking another soul's journey."

Her tone was as matter of fact as if she were describing a math exercise. I was shocked. "How can I do that to someone Joanna? That's horrible!" I felt lost in this messy world.

"Then go into the woods, you self-righteous bitch, and stay there forever." Clearly enraged, Joanna picked up a stone and threw it into the

36

woods.

For the first time, I was frightened by Joanna. I did not understand her insistence that I embark on this journey back to the Memory Pool. I couldn't see what she gained from it, but she certainly had nothing to lose. If I didn't make it, she wouldn't be affected. If I did make it, another soul would suffer. The pressure was all on me.

I asked her, "What gives you the right to force this on me? This should be my decision and my decision only. And how dare you call me a bitch!" Joanna's loss of temper made me lose mine as well. Neither of us was handling this situation well.

"You just don't understand," she said with her back to me, "and I'm sorry about that."

"Why do you care so much?" Her heightened interest in my fate continued to amaze me.

"I need some justification as to why I'm stuck here, and getting you out of this place gives me a little peace of mind. I could tell myself that I had altered someone else's course for the better." Joanna turned back around, and I could see that her hazel eyes had filled with tears.

"Perhaps," I said, "but at whose expense?" I couldn't let go of the notion that someone was going to suffer as a result of this trip through the pool.

"I understand," Joanna said, "but sometimes there's a price to pay. Yes, even here there's give and take. Maggie, you can be the giver or the taker. The choice is yours."

That sounded like an ultimatum. Ultimately, it was all Joanna had to say. And she was right. I was here, and the choice was mine.

I had Joanna elaborate a bit more on how all of this would work. It was horrifying and deceptive. We were to wait until the next soul rose from the Memory Pool. Much like I had, this soul would make its way to the shallow part of the pool and leave the water in the grassy area. I would encourage the soul to approach me by offering to help. I knew very well how scared they would be and, more importantly, how accepting they'd be of my offer to assist. My feet would be squarely placed on the dirt path as I waited for this innocent soul to come toward me. I would explain that they must not put their feet on the dirt path but stand perfectly still on the grass. I'd offer my hands as a calming gesture. I'd then step on to the grass while holding the other soul's hands. When both sets of feet were firmly on the grass and both sets of hands were connected, mayhem would ensue. Immediately a wall, similar to the wall where I had seen Reese, would rise blocking us from the dirt path, leaving only one way to proceed. I would release my hands from the other soul and sprint to the Memory Pool. Most likely, the other soul would follow with the same intensity. We'd both arrive at the pool at roughly the same time. It isn't allowed for two souls to be in the pool at the same time—and when this happens, there are consequences. One of us would make it out at the place where we'd arrived—the area known as Vulture Point—and the other of us would disappear forever. Joanna did not know where the other soul would disappear to, but she's certain that this afterlife never sees them again. That's how it would work, and now I had to decide if I'd follow through with this immoral act. I was leaning toward yes.

"Maggie, don't feel guilty about this." Joanna told me. "Remember, this is the only way you'll get closure and the last chance for you to reunite with your children." Joanna's words were precisely the justification I needed to hear.

"I'm going to do this," I told her, "but it won't be without guilt." I paced along the line where the grass met the dirt.

I'd been faced with tough decisions in my life, but nothing like this. If our plan carried out as we expected it to, I will have robbed someone of their chance for eternal happiness. I'd be replacing their needs with mine and—worse—I'd be using them as a vehicle to get what I wanted. This was beyond selfish, and I assumed that there would be consequences at some point along this journey. I felt as if I understood the good and bad consequences of this action, and I'd be going through with it anyway. I felt that I needed to be with my children. And who knows? Perhaps the soul that comes through the Memory Pool next will have been a bad person while they were alive. Of course, it wasn't going to be possible for me to know what kind of person this was when I practice my deception. But I could tell myself that I'm not robbing a good soul; I'm robbing a bad one. Yes, that will help me feel better about this act.

Once Joanna heard that I would be proceeding with her plan, she came up with the biggest grin that I've seen from her. It was clear that this was just as important to her as it was to me. Her eagerness seemed a bit odd, but then again, she was the one stuck for eternity on this path. I suppose she would be living vicariously through me. Or maybe she was just happy to provide help and to have a true purpose here. Whatever the reason, it was clear that I had a partner in crime. The terminology was appropriate. This felt like a crime in the worst way.

"Now, we wait," Joanna said, removing herself from the path so she wouldn't be visible to the poor soul that emerged next from the Memory Pool.

"What will you be doing while I go through with this?" I had a feeling that I'd be on my own.

"I can't interfere," she said. "If I touch the grass or touch either of the two of you, the pool will freeze and take all three of us with it." Joanna paused, then she added, "I've seen it happen. This is a delicate situation, and the farther away I stand, the better chance you'll have." I had the feeling that Joanna was coaching me.

The sun began to dip behind us, producing the long shadows of the kind I had seen when I first arrived. I sensed that a soul would be arriving soon, and I began to get nervous.

"I can't do this, Joanna. I can't!" My heart raced as I saw a ripple appear in the middle of the Memory Pool.

"It's time!" Joanna crouched down several feet off of the path.

The ripple turned into the familiar thrashing, with flailing arms and a torso above the water line. I couldn't get a clear view of the person coming through, but I calmed down and stood quietly along the border of the grass as this soul began to find their bearings. The thrashing became a dog paddle, and then the soul found they could stand up in the shallow portion of the pool. Then the soul was inching through the water, approaching the safety of the shore. The sun was rising but hadn't made its way above the cliff, so it was still dark, and I had a hard time seeing my opponent. I had decided to view this encounter as a competition—a competition with more than just a victory at stake. I simply had to pump myself up for this confrontation. I felt like a boxer waiting in the ring for my opponent to emerge from the locker room. All that was missing was the walkout music blaring from the loudspeakers. I could feel my calmness giving way to a kind of blood lust.

The soul stepped forward onto the grass, and suddenly the image was in focus. It was a man, a man standing about six-foot-four with a chiseled physique. He looked to be in his twenties. Panic began to run through me when I realized that this was the person I would have to beat in a dead sprint to the pool. Of the two of us, he was by far the better

39

athlete! My strategy was going to need to change to give me any chance of pulling this off. His naivety would be his downfall. I'd win this challenge not with brawn, but with my brain.

The man strode through the grass in my direction with a confidence that made me wonder if he had been here before. His white undershirt did little to cover his bulging chest and biceps. His bottom half was covered with a pair of jeans and of course, he was barefoot. A silent Joanna remained crouched down off the path, awaiting the confrontation.

He was less than a hundred feet away when I first locked eyes with him. I lifted my right arm then and started waving him in. I may have looked self-assured, but at that point, my heart was pounding, and my confidence began to falter. I felt intimidated. I kept saying to myself, "Use your mind. Use your mind." But I knew I couldn't turn back now, so I took a took a deep breath and did what I felt I needed to do.

"Hello," I called to him, continuing to wave my arm to flag him down.

My greeting went unanswered. This soul kept marching forward, moving aggressively. He was about thirty feet away now, and I could see a smile on his face. He looked at me, and then he looked down at his feet, which were steadily propelling him closer to me.

"This must be Heaven!" he shouted, and he grinned at me as he took his final steps toward me—arriving right where I needed him to be.

"Not quite Heaven," I said to him, "but we're close." I returned his smile with a smile of my own, although what was behind my smile was at least some fear.

"Oh, this must be Heaven," he said. "Look at me!" He jumped up and down, kicking each of his legs out in front of him, and then he patted his quads.

"Be careful," I said. His excitement had almost taken him onto the dirt path.

"Be careful? Hey, I'm dead already, right?" He bent down to feel his toes, running his hands over both feet.

"Yeah, but you have to be careful here. You don't know anything about this place." I acted like I was a seasoned veteran.

"All I know is that I'm walking again. I have my legs!" He once again bounced up and down and even twirled around in the air performing a complete 360.

40

"Now, that's cool!" I couldn't help but smile at that. This was such a special moment for this soul—and he had inspired two completely spontaneous smiles in me in the few minutes that I'd known him. He was bringing some happiness to this dark place! I appreciated that, but I remembered what I was here to do. So, I immediately got down to the business of deception.

"I can help you," I told him. "I've been here for a while, and I've figured this place out. You're not in Heaven, but, like I said, you're close," I pointed over his shoulder back toward the Memory Pool.

"Then where are we now?" he asked. "I kind of like it right here. Look around. That's the greenest grass I've ever seen, and those trees— look at those yellow flowers!" His head was spinning.

I needed to rain a bit on his parade. "You're not in Heaven," I said. "I can tell you that for sure."

It was obvious that this man had lost his legs during his life and that those legs had been given back to him in the afterlife. While I was curious to learn how he had lost them, I had several reasons for not wanting to open up too much of a conversation with him. First, I needed to concentrate on my task at hand and, second, if I learned too much about him, I might not be able to follow through with my plan. I already felt connected to this guy, and the stronger that connection became, the guiltier I would feel about what I was planning to do to him.

"Twenty-two years! Twenty-two!" He was hopping up and down. He was so thrilled to be able to use his legs that he just couldn't contain himself. When he finally settled down, his raw emotions took over and he began to cry. Then he knelt, running his hands over his toes and feet with tears dropping onto the grass. When he raised his face again, I was once again greeted with his brilliant smile. The positivity he'd been able to bring to this negative world was   refreshing and a bit contagious.

"So, it's been twenty-two years since you were able to walk," I said. "That's really something!" I smiled at him, and I meant it.

There was some kind of inconsistency in this story, but I knew that, in this messy place, looks can be deceiving. This man looked to be in his twenties, but I knew he probably wasn't. Now, a consistency in this messy place has been that looks are deceiving, and since he only looked to be in his twenties, I had to assume that he didn't lose his legs as a toddler.

I asked him, "How old were you when you died?" I couldn't help myself.

"Fifty-one. Cancer got me," he said without hesitation.

"And how about the legs, what happened there?"

"Iraq, roadside bomb. Almost died then, too, but they couldn't get the rest of me. Took cancer to finish me off."

"Well, you're here now," I said, "And there's a reason for that. But that's for you to find out, not me." I was feeling agitated, and he picked up on that.

"I thought you said you can help me?" He finally looked as though he was taking this situation seriously.

"Oh, I can help you"—that was a lie—"but you'll need to help yourself, too." The truth was that I had no intention of helping anyone but myself.

"What's your name, sweetheart?"

"Maggie—and you?"

"Alphonso, but they call me Phonso." He turned his back to me then, taking a moment to see where he had come from, looking in particular at the height of the cliff.

I knew what was running through his head. "It felt like it was a lot higher, didn't it?"

"Hell, yeah!" He swiveled his head around and smiled at me again! "I've jumped out of planes, but that cliff jump was as intense as anything I've ever experienced."

I couldn't help but wonder if I had any other options. Did it have to be me versus him? But I was in no position to sneak over to Joanna for advice. Would it matter? I was sure she would tell me to follow through with the plan. I was also sure that Phonso had loved ones who were waiting for him on the other side of this mess and that I would be the only roadblock keeping that reunion from becoming a reality. In that sense, I was worse than Cliff! Yes, Cliff had physically ended our lives, but as far as I'm aware, he didn't steal our souls.

Phonso continued to enjoy the rebirth of his legs, jogging back and forth, sometimes giving way to a full out sprint. It was easy to see why he thought this was Heaven, but little did he know, it was about to become Hell. His smile, his story, none of it mattered to me. I was about to commit the most selfish act I'd ever committed, and I was OK with it. It was time to find my children, even at the expense of this Phonso.

"Are you ready?" I placed my feet on the edge of the dirt path with my hands out.

"As ready as I'll ever be, right?" He laughed and walked forward with his hands positioned to meet mine.

"OK, now stop right there," I motioned to an area in the grass that was approximately a foot away from me. It was close enough for us to grab each other's hands, but far enough to allow me to step on to the grass.

This entire plan hinged on what I had heard from Joanna. I had no direct knowledge of what was about to happen. I thought I needed to win a sprint against Phonso, and that seemed like an insurmountable task. Then it struck me: *He doesn't know this is a race. He's following my lead because I'm the so-called expert here.* I decided to take another route with my deception, one that would guarantee my reaching the pool first.

"Now, listen carefully," I told him. "When we lock arms, things will get a little crazy around here, but don't panic. All you'll need to do is follow me down to the pool. I'll lead the way, and we'll be alright." I think he bought it. Why wouldn't he?

"Well, OK then, let's do this." Phonso held his arms out, and I took a deep breath.

I noticed a tattoo on his right forearm with the words *Semper Fi*. This Marine had lived a tough life, and I was about to make his afterlife tougher than anything he'd experienced while alive.

"One, two, three!" I yelled as I stared into Phonso's eyes.

I stepped forward onto the grass as we locked arms with only about five inches between us. We were almost hugging. I saw the fear in his eyes, which startled me. His confident demeanor disappeared as the weight of the moment took over. He gripped my arms tighter, but I felt no pain. I continued to stare into his eyes as our serene surroundings began to disappear. The grass turned brown while the yellow flowers on the trees dropped off, also turning brown the instant they reached the ground. The wind blew violently, unsettling the calmness of the Memory Pool. I glanced around Phonso's shoulder to take a better look. The pool looked like it was boiling over. Massive bubbles were rising from below and exploding as they reached the surface. Screams were flowing out of the pool producing a horrible shrieking that blasted right through my ears. I'd never heard such a painful sound. It continued to get louder, causing Phonso and me to shout at one another.

"What do we do? What do we do?" His grip tightened.

I lifted my right leg and stepped past Phonso's left leg, almost falling into him. As my foot hit the brown dying grass, it happened. Suddenly, Phonso fell to the ground. Our arms were still interlocked, but he was on the ground staring up at me helplessly. His legs were gone. The brief joy he had experienced being able to walk again was gone, and I was the reason this had happened. As much as it pained me to see him struggle on the ground, I freed my hands from his and began my sprint to the bubbling pool. He screamed for me, but I ignored him, never looking back. I couldn't look at him again. It was too painful.

The water from the Memory Pool combined with the fierce wind to produce a mist that met my skin as I continued my sprint away from Phonso. His wailing continued, and it pierced right through my body. I arrived at the edge of the pool, allowing the waves to crash onto my toes. The water was hot, much like a Jacuzzi would produce, but the color was a faint orange. I knelt down, placing my hands in the water. Not only was it orange, but it was coarse. So coarse, I was able to rub the particles in between my fingers and flick them back into the water. Phonso's wailing turned into a direct scream aimed at me.

"Why did you do this to me? Come back! Please help me!" His screams failed to turn me around. I wasn't going to look back at him.

The water began to flatten out as the wind ceased, but the orange appearance remained. Phonso's wailing and screaming also stopped. My curiosity got the best of me, and I turned around. To my surprise, Phonso was no longer there. The grass turned green again, and the yellow flowers on the trees reappeared. Everything looked exactly as it had prior to my stepping on the grass. I was alone on the shore contemplating my next steps. I knew what I needed to do, but found it difficult to take the plunge back into the pool. All of this required tremendous faith in Joanna. While she seemed trustworthy, I didn't know for sure what her motives were and her overenthusiastic interest in my situation seemed a bit odd. Once again, my mental state was being challenged, and the exhaustion from these recent events had taken its toll. I sat down, both feet in the water, grasping my knees and resting my head on my arms, staring across the pool to the cliff. I didn't see the point in rushing through this process, and my break gave me a good excuse to let go. I sat by the pool with tears pouring down my cheeks, hitting the sandy ground below me. These are the moments here that I've learned to hate. When I'm given time to reflect, I get depressed. Most of my time here has been spent trying to figure out my next move, which has not allowed me to dwell on my past, present, or future.

CHAPTER SIX

I miss my kids. I miss my life and wish everything could return to normal. It's easy to fondly remember the big events in my life like my wedding or the births of my children, but it's the small things that mean the most. I specifically remember a Friday night in October. It was the Friday just before Halloween. We chose to stay home and make it a game night with some pizza. Our whole family sat around the kitchen table, playing cards and board games while devouring a couple of pizzas. The boys enjoyed their "everything" pies, while Reese and I kept it simple with cheese—well, extra cheese. Cliff and I let the kids stay up past midnight, which was also an accomplishment for the two of us, as we rarely made it much past ten. The laughter was nonstop, and there were no arguments, which was a small miracle. I don't remember the games we played, but I do remember the smiles on all of our faces. Ben had just gotten a new phone, and he Snapchatted our night. I still have no idea how to use Snapchat, but Ben had fun with it.

As quickly as those photos disappeared, so did our beautiful lives. I met Brent the following night, and things went downhill from there. To this day, I don't know why I strayed. I suppose it was just the adventure of it all. Cliff and I were in such a routine—a routine that lacked intimacy. We had fun with each other and with the kids, but we were more like a team than we were a husband and wife. We were a well-oiled machine when it came to running our household, but operating like an appliance isn't exactly the recipe for a successful marriage. I believe we both used the kids as an excuse for not addressing the problems we had with each other. There was an elephant in the room, but we chose to ignore it. The path of least resistance was to turn our heads away and dive into whatever the kids had going on in their lives at the moment.

To simplify this, Brent made me feel pretty again. Yes, the sex was different, and I craved the novelty because of the lack of any newness at home. I think it was more about feeling good about myself. Cliff was never derogatory in relation to my looks, but he never acknowledged me in that way at all. I'd get my hair done, and he wouldn't notice. I'd commit to working out and eating right—and there would be results. Not the type of results you see on infomercials, but I did look better. Cliff wouldn't say a word. He didn't *see* any difference. I don't think he saw me at all. I received more compliments from my children than from my husband. Reese was always there to tell Mommy that she looked pretty. Even the boys would throw compliments my way, although their delivery could have used some work.

It was very different with Brent. He constantly complimented me—on the phone, by text, in person. We had found each other during rough patches in both of our marriages. His wife had a sharp-tongued way of making him feel like shit. He didn't provide well enough for her. She sat on her ass at home, while he did what he could to live up to her expectations. It was never good enough for her. So, I was an escape for Brent in the same way that he was an escape for me. The two of us were living in our fantasy world, thinking that this indulgence wasn't going to affect anyone but ourselves. To give ourselves some credit   though—most trysts like ours end in divorce, not murder.

In the afterlife, the sun continues to rise and set, but not in a dependable twenty-four hour cycle. I haven't yet figured out any consistent cycle. Sometimes the sun will hover in one spot for an extended period of time, and then it will disappear, surrendering to the moon for another inconsistent period of time. The moon has been full, crescent, and half, but in no particular order. This is just another question for which I have no answer. I'm starting to lose track as to how long I've been here and perhaps that's the point. I guess the concept of time is irrelevant when all things are eternal. Monty told me that the moment I arrived, and I'm beginning to understand what he meant by this. How many times the sun rises and sets here doesn't matter. What matters is the end game. I haven't been able to determine exactly what my end game is—other than my own goal of making sure I reunite with my kids. I've tried to make that happen, and so far, I've failed.

The mental break I took on the shore of the Memory Pool was sorely needed. Since sleeping is not an option here, these mental breaks are the only way I've been able to refresh myself. At this point, though, I had procrastinated long enough. I stood up, determined to take the next steps into the pool. Darkness was now upon me, but once again, the moon provided enough light so that I could clearly see across the pool to the cliff. I turned around taking a glance at the path as well. All clear.

I gingerly placed my right foot into the pool. I stopped before bringing my left foot forward. Each step can have a substantial impact, therefore I was careful not to proceed too quickly. I had one foot in, and the pool remained calm. I brought my left foot forward. Both feet were now in the calm pool, ankle deep. Again, everything remained calm. Except for the ripple I was making by getting into it, the pool looked like a sheet of glass.

Step by step, I continued, and to my surprise the pool and the rest of my surroundings remained placid. The water was up to my chin now as I was standing on my tip toes. I began to swim to the center of the pool. The temperature of the water was delightful, like a warm bath. I reached my destination without issue; I kept treading water and looking for some kind of sign. What was I supposed to do next? I looked all around but nothing revealed itself—not in the pool, on the cliff, at the shore, or even on the path in the distance. The cycle of the sun and the moon came and went three times while I treaded water in the center of the pool. Still there was nothing. Had I done something wrong? I had followed Joanna's instructions to the letter. Of course, what was supposed to be a race with Phonso hadn't been that at all. Still, I had won. I'd beat him to the pool, which was what I was told to do.

Now, I was running out of patience. I decided to return to the shore. Maybe the best step now would be to find Joanna and figure out what had gone wrong. I swam toward the shore, arriving at the spot where I remembered the pool being shallow enough for me to stand. To my surprise, I was unable to touch the bottom here. I stretched my legs down, and my head went briefly under the water. I shook the water from my face, swam forward some more, and tried again. Still, I was unable to touch the bottom. I was only fifteen feet from the shore, but still, I couldn't touch bottom. The depth of the pool must have changed. I swam some more, but the fifteen-foot distance remained constant. I wasn't getting any closer. I knew I was moving forward as I swam, which meant the shore was moving away from me at an equal speed. I floated for a bit before trying again. The same thing happened. I was not allowed to leave the pool.

The temperature of the water dropped quickly. My warm bath turned bitterly cold. My teeth began to chatter as the water became increasingly difficult to move in. It occurred to me that this pool could freeze over. Everything might turn to ice, including me. My kicking slowed, and so did my breathing. I managed to get back to the center of the pool, but that's where my efforts would stall. While I wasn't exactly frozen, I could barely move. My efforts were useless. I tried to lift my arm out of what was once water and failed. My head still moved freely, but I could only see to the left, right and in front of me. It was impossible to move around.

Off in the distance where the water met the cliff, I noticed something odd: a small wave began to form, looking as if it had bounced off the cliff and the momentum of this was taking it back in my direction. The swell was only about five feet across and about that long. I wondered if perhaps someone, or something, wasn't directly underneath this wave, causing it to happen. The water around me began to warm again, allowing me to free myself from what was almost a frozen state. The swell approached slowly, remaining the same size. It arrived only fifteen feet from me and began to swirl around in place, creating an intense whirlpool. The current pulled me forward and, rather than panicking, I let my body go. This was the first sign I'd received on what to do next—and this option seemed as good as any.

The current took me very rapidly into this tightly formed whirlpool. As it swallowed me, I took a deep breath as I began what seemed like a slow freefall in which I was being submerged in the water of the Memory Pool. I have no idea how far I traveled, but it was clear that I moved on from the grassy area with the pretty flowers and Joanna and the Path of Lost Souls. I was falling feet-first. I noticed that I was approaching the end of the whirlpool as all light began to disappear, leaving me underwater in complete darkness. I placed my hand out to touch the interior of the whirlpool. The water was moving so aggressively around me that my fingers bounced off of the interior. The water actually scraped my fingers, feeling much like road rash. There was no going up or out to the side. My only choice was to continue my descent into the black.

Finally, my knees buckled as I violently arrived at what I assumed to be the bottom of the Memory Pool—or at least the end of this awful ride. I rose from the bottom, pushing myself up with my hands, immediately noticing the slick surface of whatever I had landed on. I waved my hand directly in front of my face. My eyes were open, but couldn't see my hand. I was in a spot where light could not travel. I had no choice but to wait for whatever was coming next. And then it happened.

My feet became firmly planted in a slick surface below them. I tried to step forward, but I couldn't pick up either foot. The water began to rush upward, and there was a glimmer of light, which allowed me to gain some idea as to what was happening. I was completely dry with my feet still firmly locked to the surface below me. I looked up to see the entire Memory Pool hovering above me. Hundreds of souls appeared in the pool, struggling to push their way up to the surface. The grip on my feet loosened then, and a path appeared in front of me. It was made of the same slick surface; it looked like black quartz. I proceeded cautiously along the path, noticing a sliver of light about five hundred feet ahead. The light was almost flickering. It would disappear and then come back again, but there was enough light that I could make out a bit of what was around me.

I was walking along the path. As I proceeded, I saw that fine sand was pouring down through a small hole. The hole was about six inches wide. When the hole was covered, no light got through. Then the sand would drop, the hole would open up, and light would come again. This hole was about seven feet above the quartz path. It was my way out. Where it would end, I did not know. But it was clearly my only option for a way forward.

I was now at the hole and watching the sand fall down to the quartz path. I stood just over five feet, and the hole was seven feet high. Clearly, there was nothing around to stand on, and my only choice was to wait for enough sand to pile up below to give me the desired lift I needed to start digging at the six-inch hole so that I could make it wide enough to allow me to escape. The sand would pour out, then stop. I watched for what seemed like hours until finally, the sand reached a level where I could successfully stand on it and reach my hand in and around the hole.

I started to hit away at the sides of the hole, expanding it steadily. This wouldn't take long now. I could see that I'd be free soon. Of course, I didn't know what this "freedom" meant; I didn't know what was waiting for me on the other side. When the hole was about double in size, with sand continuing to fall through it, I realized that I was going to move quickly. There was only about two and a half feet of space left under the hole. The space would soon be full. I decided to take a chance, and I raised one arm through the hole, hoping to find something to grab hold of on the other side. If I could secure myself to something, I could pull myself through.

Then I felt something catch hold of me—and yank my arm. My head burst through the hole, and moments later I found myself lying on my back in a daze. The sky was clear above me, and the sun was shining. I had been removed from the hole. Everything felt familiar, and for good reason. When I opened my eyes and looked around, I saw   in front of me, my old friend Monty.

He was not smiling. "What the fuck do you think you're doing?" he said. I tried to get up, and he pushed me back down.

"Hey, get off of me!" I managed to kneel and to brush the hair out of my face.

Monty was clearly furious. "Who told you to go back in the pool?" he asked me, and he was talking at full volume.

"You have no right to yell at me," I told him. "And keep your hands to yourself." I stepped back two steps to create some space between us.

"I do have the right," Monty said. "I've earned it. Now, tell me, who told you to go back in the pool?" He took two steps toward me, closing the gap once again.

"Her name was Joanna. I met her on the path."

Monty's anger deflated when I mentioned Joanna's name. Was he afraid? I couldn't tell.

"What else did Joanna do to you?"

"What do you mean—do to me? She didn't do anything to me." Suddenly, everything looked different to me. It seemed that Monty didn't trust Joanna, and if he didn't, how could I? Had I been trusting the wrong person?

"You need to tell me everything," Monty said, taking hold of my right forearm and squeezing it. "If you don't, then that's it. I'm walking away."

"OK," I said. "I will, but let go of me." I pried my arm loose, but as I did, I began to share everything that had happened to me since I'd last seen Monty. I wasn't very far into my story before it was apparent to me that I'd put my trust in the wrong person—someone with their own agendas. It was quite clear that I knew nothing about this place, and not only were others I'd met along the way a danger to me, but I was becoming a danger to myself.

Monty asked me, "Remember when I mentioned PopCon to you?"

"Yes, but you never told me anything about it. What does that mean?"

"I didn't tell you more about it," Monty said, "because I was trying to sniff you out. I wasn't sure if you were one of them yourself." His reasoning sounded logical, but heightened my curiosity.

"Well, I'm not," I said. "So, can you tell me what it is?"

"It's Population Control—or PopCon for short. They are the ones responsible for your death."

"My death? How could that be?" My heart raced waiting to hear his explanation.

"They are responsible for everyone that dies. Doesn't matter how or who you are, PopCon did it." This was preposterous to me, but Monty was saying it with perfect confidence.

"What about God?" I leaned on what I had learned going to church all of those years.

"God is waiting for you on the other side. You were denied entry for some reason, which you'll most likely figure out at some point. God has to do with life and how you live life. It's PopCon that brings death."

Having crushed my most cherished beliefs in just a couple of sentences, Monty continued to supply detail after detail about PopCon. It turned out that many lost souls do just what I had done—working as a puppet for PopCon or stepping in and joining them in their work. The Path of Lost Souls is actually not full of a million lost souls like Joanna claimed. The majority of those souls end up with PopCon contributing in some manner to the heartbreak that continuously occurs on Earth. Whether it's innocent babies succumbing to cancer or hardened criminals dying due to their own negligence, it all stems from PopCon. Joanna actually functions as a recruiter—although her motive with me probably wasn't recruitment. I think she used me as a pawn. Maybe there was some reason she needed to get to Phonso. Maybe she wanted to watch me perform. It was hard to say.

"What do you think Joanna wanted from me?" I asked Monty. "She didn't try to recruit me."

"That, I don't know," he said, "but it will reveal itself soon enough." What I could see is that Monty was on a mission against PopCon. I figured that was why he was stuck here. He'd fight the tough battle helping souls like me become free from PopCon's grip.

Population Control occupied the space that Monty pointed out as six o'clock when he originally mapped out this world to me. We were back with the vultures now, which seemed to be Monty's home base.

"Now," he said with purpose, "we need to figure out what your next steps are."

It was hard for me to let go of what I had done. "I'm afraid that I've set some things in motion here that I shouldn't have," I said. "I wish I would have seen through Joanna." Hurting Phonso the way I had was weighing on me.

Monty comforted me. "What's done is done," he said. "It's time to move forward. I'll help you where I can, but you'll be on your own as well."

"So, what's next? Please don't tell me I have to go back to the Memory Pool. I've had enough of that place." I was smiling as I said this, but my words were only half in jest. The truth is that I was terrified of the Memory Pool.

Monty was walking as we talked, and now we arrived at the same clearing where he mapped out this crazy, in between world that we both presently called home. It was easy to feel sorry for Monty after all he's experienced both in life and death, but another feeling began to arise in me. I felt envy. Monty knew what his purpose was here. He was having an impact; he was helping lost souls like me achieve closure. By contrast, all I've been doing was bouncing around here with no plan and no notion where I'll end up—with Hell being a possible final destination.

Monty was still trying to help me figure out my next move. He asked me, "You didn't go anywhere else, did you?"

"No, just through the pool and down the path and then got rejected."

"Tell me everything," he said. "Every detail is important and crucial to your next steps." Monty seemed to be accusing me of not being forthright.

"That's what happened. That's all of it!" I didn't like the feeling that I was being interrogated.

"Other than Joanna and the Marine, who else did you run into along the way?"

Then I remembered. "There was one other person—a terrible boy who acted like a grown man. He hit me," I said, "and he knew my whole story. He knew exactly how I died." Just thinking about the encounter with him made me tremble again.

"Where did you see him?"

"He arrived on the shore of the Memory Pool shortly after me."

"Then what happened?" Monty was pressing me for more information.

"He was there, smacked me to the ground and threatened me. He ran off to the path, and I haven't seen him since."

"I've never heard of anyone here matching that description. He came to you for a reason, and his knowledge of your past tells me he must be with PopCon. We need to find him again." Monty said the words I didn't want to hear.

"No, I can't do it. Monty, please!" I pleaded. "There must be another way."

"Your way out of here goes through him," Monty said. "I'm sure of it."

"I'm not ready to go back there. I can't do it, Monty." Once again, I was pleading, but I was thinking more of the Memory Pool. I didn't want to go back into that pool.

"You don't have to go back now," Monty said. "Actually, you can't go back now anyway. Eventually you'll have to if you want to see your kids again. For now, we have some more tests ahead of us." Monty walked over to the clearing and began scribbling in the dirt with a stick.

He drew the familiar circle with the cross inside of it. I already knew what nine o'clock was all about and Monty introduced me to six o'clock and the nastiness that went on there. Three o'clock and twelve o'clock were still mysteries.

"So, tell me about three and twelve," I asked, knowing that I wouldn't like the answers.

"Twelve and three," he said, reversing the numbers. "Both are necessary stops for you, although three could easily be your last."

"Three my last, why?" The obvious question.

"Well, because three is Hell. If you pass through there, nothing else really matters, and from the sound of your past, that might just be where you end up." Monty laughed then, and his amusement got on my nerves.

"Why do you seem to take joy in this?" My voice cut right through what I saw as sinister laughter.

"Settle down," he said. "I don't make the rules here; I just play by them. Forgive me for enjoying this a little more than I should, but it's my way of staying sane. You'll be leaving, one way or the other, and I'll stay on here in the netherworld. I so rarely find something to smile at. And I mean no harm to you when I do." Monty caught hold of my hand and squeezed it gently, looking at me with his kind eyes.

I took a deep breath and looked over his shoulder to the east, knowing that my fate was awaiting me. "How do we get there?" I asked.

"Now, that's the attitude we need!" Monty said with a grin.

CHAPTER SEVEN

Before we started marching east, Monty provided me with crucial information, as he needed full buy in. He explained how everything and everyone here is connected in some way. His role was somewhat unique in that most of the others had some kind of endgame in mind. It would be easy to think that everyone here wanted one result, to pass through to Heaven, but that was far from reality. Motivation and goals here functioned similarly to the way they did when we were all alive. We're all individuals with different agendas, some good and some bad. Our actions speak the loudest, and just like we are held accountable for what we do in life, the same goes for death. In other words, I didn't have a clean slate when I arrived here, and just like I was being judged for what I did while I was alive, I'm being judged in death. Once again, my sense of guilt for what I had done to Phonso came roaring back. It would be easy for me to blame Joanna for what had happened, but it was my actions that caused Phonso's pain, not Joanna's. Alive and dead, I'm causing harm to others. Maybe Hell is exactly where I belong. This trip east was another of the tests along the way, the most crucial one yet. As Monty said, if I pass through there, nothing else matters.

"How many have you seen pass through to Hell?" I asked, hoping to hear that it's very rare.

"Too many." Monty gave a simple answer to a complex question.

"Too many?"

"I've lost count." Monty did nothing to diminish my fear.

"Why didn't you help them?" I was frustrated with Monty's nonchalant manner.

"Seriously? Now, you're questioning me? Show some fucking respect! Ever since I met you, your attitude has been shitty. Maybe if you stop thinking about yourself for one second, you'll start figuring out how things work here." I could tell that Monty was once again on the brink of leaving me to fend for myself.

"Sorry," I said. "It's the thought of Hell—an eternity in Hell! Who is prepared for that? Believe me, it's not that I don't respect you or what you do here."

Monty seemed to relax then. "Not that I need to justify myself," he said, "but for the record, I try to save everyone I meet here. In my mind, the past is the past. Unfortunately, that's not how it works. Here, the past means everything. The past dictates your future. So, it's always too late for me to help when I meet souls like you out here. The decision on whether you'll pass through to Hell has already been made. I just try to make it easier for you while you go down the path. That's all I can offer. You can accept my help or walk away."

Monty turned his back to me then; he was looking toward the east because, of course, that's where we needed to go.

Monty and I began our march to the east in silence. I was thinking about what might be awaiting me at the end of this walk. Memories of my entire life were vivid in my mind, all the way back to when I was a toddler. The memories were slowly rolling through my brain. They were so clear that I was experiencing them all over again. As these memories rolled through, a theme began to develop. These were the sins I had committed throughout my lifetime. From the time I stole a pack of gum from the convenience store when I was eight years old, to my first time masturbating, and ending up with the infidelity that resulted in the murder of me and my children. The inventory that I was presented with was amazing and, at the same time, terrifying. Every detail of every sin— sin as it had been defined by my church—was brought forward for me to analyze and relive. There were the obvious transgressions, the ones that had consumed me with guilt at the time, and there were also others that hadn't seemed like a big deal. Yes, I've cursed quite a bit in my life, but is that really a sin? I'd never thought so, but maybe the extremists were right and maybe now I'd be paying for every minor sin I ever committed—as well as the major sins, of course.

Shuffling through all of these blemishes I'd made in my lifetime required a long walk. When I was finally done reliving all of my wrongs, I had arrived at a rapidly flowing river. This river was shallow but wide, and it had rocks spread throughout. Monty was still by my side. It was unclear to me as to how far we had walked or how long it had taken. I've had a hard time accepting the idea that the concept of time is irrelevant here. It's natural to want to place a time on events, creating a beginning, middle and end, but that's better left for the living, not the dead. I would be faced with my personal eternity soon. I just hoped it wasn't an eternity spent in Hell.

"Looks like you made it through OK. I've definitely seen worse," Monty said with a small smile.

"What do you mean?" I asked him.

"You've led a pretty good life," he said. "A few mistakes here and there, but like I said, I've seen worse." Monty walked over to the edge of the river and, bending down, dipped one hand in the rough water.

"You saw everything, didn't you?" I felt ashamed and embarrassed knowing that Monty knew everything about me. Well, the bad things anyway.

"I did." Monty got up, rubbing his hands together as the water dripped down his forearms. "That's how it works," he said.

Consistency in one's life tends to soothe the mind. I had been trying to find consistency in the afterlife, but the only constant I'd experienced here is the beauty and mystery of this place. I wasn't well traveled while I was living, and perhaps that's why what I'd seen here had left me awestruck. The crisp, brightness of the colors, the beauty of the trees and grass—it's all been a pleasant distraction. Sometimes I'd   find myself mesmerized by a random leaf dangling from a tree, staring at the deep green and its clearly delineated patterns. These moments have helped ease my pain and give my mind the break it needs to carry on in a world that is completely inconsistent.

I sat down next to the rushing waters of the river, looking at each rock that broke the surface. Some rocks were smooth, others were jagged. The river ran from south to north with no end in sight. While looking at a river's currents from the bank, it's easy to assume the flowing water would be easy to navigate. The real danger, however, lies underneath the surface, where hidden currents can pull your body into obstacles—like these very rocks. From the shore, the Memory Pool had appeared to be serene; only after you'd become immersed in that pool did its true nature become clear. Right now, the sound of the water flowing by could lull a person to sleep, but I knew that this river was nothing to take lightly. Monty hadn't brought me here to halt my journey at the water's edge. I knew my fate would be determined in the river itself.

Then I realized that I had been focused on my own wellbeing without giving a thought to what might be ahead for Monty. I turned to him and asked, "Where do you think you'll end up?"

Monty gave another little smile. "I'll tell you this," he said. "Every time I think I have this place figured out, I get thrown a curveball. Just like you, I hope I find eternal peace, but the more vultures I see, the more I start to accept that my fate may be just this: helping people like you."

"What do you want?" I asked him. It's a complex question for anyone. Monty sat down beside me on the riverbank before he answered.

"The same thing I've wanted since I was a little kid. I just want to be happy. Happiness has forever eluded me. I had dreams: I wanted to marry, have my own family, perhaps a son. I never had any of those, so I left the world incomplete."

Monty had wanted exactly what I'd had. Happiness never eluded me or my family, which again brings up the question of why I had cheated on my husband when I had everything already? Selfishness? Stubbornness? Or maybe I just became a mean person. Whatever it was, it was wrong, and the worst of this was I had known it was the wrong thing to do all along. And I had the ability to right my wrongs, but I hadn't done that. Sitting next to Monty, who'd already told me all about his painful past, only fueled my pain and guilt. I was sitting on the doorstep of Hell, and if the decision were mine, I'd probably send myself there. I don't know if this decision was mine to make, but if it were, in this moment I'd take my medicine and accept responsibility for my three dead children—not to mention the living one, Ben, who was left with a father in jail and a dead mother. The similarities between Monty's past and Ben's present were uncanny. I could only hope Ben didn't take the path Monty had taken, ending his own life. I hoped Ben's sadness could somehow turn to happiness.

"My son Ben was the one left behind," I said aloud to Monty. "Ben's got a tough road ahead of him—like you had."

"How old was he?"

"Seventeen, just started driving, and he loved every minute of that." I remembered fondly the day Ben had passed his driver's test.

"Going through what Ben went through is tough no matter what age," Monty said. "But seventeen is just what I was when my parents were taken from me. It's an especially awkward age—you're almost an adult, but you're really still a kid. Other people have expectations of you that are all over the place. Some want to baby you, and others want to treat you like a man."

All of this was enlightening and helpful for me to hear. I asked Monty, "And how do you think Ben should be treated?"

"Not like I was," he said. "My relatives chose to treat me like I was a man. They acted like nothing had happened to my parents. I was into the Army before I ever had a chance to grieve." Monty paused for a moment. "Actually, I never have grieved."

That was horrifying, but I was still focused on my son. "I wish I knew how Ben was doing," I said. "He's living with Cliff's brother and sister-in-law now. I hope they aren't making the same mistakes your family made. Ben probably won't be going into the military, but college is just around the corner. Maybe he should stay at home and go to a junior college for now." I realized that my recommendation—valid though it was—was being heard only by Monty. It wasn't going to do Ben any good at all.

"I wish I could speak to Ben," I said.

"There is a way, you know," Monty turned his head away from the river and our eyes met.

"For me to speak to Ben?" Adrenaline rushed through me.

"To speak to anyone," Monty said. "I can't say that I've personally experienced doing this, but I've been with others who have."

"I need to do this, Monty," I stood, still looking him in the eye. "Can you help me?"

"I shouldn't have said anything." Monty got up and walked a few paces from the river. "I didn't want to get your hopes up, but I guess it's too late to worry about that."

"Just tell me how it's done. I'll do it myself, if you'll just tell me what to do."

I had forgotten about Monty's mood swings—and that he wasn't someone who handled demands especially well. "You are a real pushy bitch," he said in his no-nonsense voice. "Don't you tell me how this is coming down! You don't know anything about this place, so don't go thinking you can do anything alone."

Monty paused for a second to let that sink in. Then he went on.

"Don't forget that I'm all you've got out here. I leave, and it's good luck to you. I have something that you don't have right now and that's knowledge. I hold the cards. Stop forgetting that!"

As startled as I was by his aggressive tone, I knew he was right. I had nothing and knew nothing. Without Monty I was lost. The mistakes I'd made here had all happened when Monty wasn't with me. His yelling did exactly what I believe he intended it to do, I was completely intimidated. Once again, my stubbornness had proven to be a detriment rather than an advantage. I did the only thing I could do, I apologized.

"I'm sorry," I said. "I just got excited at the thought of connecting with my family. I guess that's what matters most to me."

Monty's blood pressure had cooled enough that he could launch into another lesson—how to understand this world we were in. This time I hung on every word.

He asked me, "How many vultures did you see when you arrived? I bet there were three, right?"

I thought back. "Yes," I said. "How did you know that?"

"This isn't meant to be a test, but what do you think the significance is of three vultures?"

I told him that I was stumped. I hadn't given any thought at all to the number of vultures I'd seen.

"I thought you might have figured it out," Monty said. "But I realize that's asking a lot under the circumstances. You saw one vulture for each of your three deceased children. I think that's why there were three."

Monty explained that he had watched countless souls arrive at Vulture Point. Some come with multiple vultures circling while others have none at all. He'd learned that the level of pain a soul has endured is proportionate to the number of vultures flying above that soul. "Three is a lot," he said. "One or two is common, but anything beyond that usually means the soul has a lot of pain to release." He said that once he saw the three vultures, he took a special interest in my situation. It turned out he'd only assisted six others with three vultures or more. The most was seven vultures.

He was a little sheepish when he admitted that he has a special interest when he sees three or more vultures because he knows a significant challenge lies ahead. And, more importantly, he knows that he needs to get to this soul before Population Control can pollute them. Monty said that he leaves Vulture Point only when he's with a three-plus vulture soul. Of course, while he's gone, he might miss some other arrivals, but the reward had always seemed greater than the risk. Until someone arrives to help, which is unlikely, he said he's content to miss some of the opportunities.

"Out of six," he said, "I've lost only one. You're lucky number seven, so let's not let anything bad happen to you." He winked.

I didn't like that wink. "Lost one?" I said. "What does that mean?"

"Lost to PopCon. I'm out here battling those fuckers all alone," Monty added. "Fuck them."

"What happened to the one you lost?" I wasn't going to be number two.

"We both made mistakes," Monty admitted. "And I haven't made another mistake since. It was my first and my naivete got the best of me."

Monty explained that he saw many souls come and go at the Vulture Point, but this person, Marshall, was the first to have had three vultures. Instinct told Monty to take a special interest in this soul. Much like I was when I'd met Monty, Marshall had been lost, scared, vulnerable, and not at all trusting. As the story unfolded, Monty and Marshall began to connect by going through the circumstances of Marshall's life. Ironically, they had gone through their childhoods at the same time and not far from one another, both having lived just outside of Philadelphia, though on opposite ends. As a teenager Marshall ran with a tough crowd and became a part of the area's seedy criminal world. He lived in Chester, though he didn't spend a lot of time there. He'd sleep on friends' couches, staying in the city and going home only once in a while, when he felt guilty for ignoring his parents. Every time he'd visit his parents, they'd greet him with open arms, hoping that this time he would stay and turn his life around. His disappearing acts made them angry, but once he showed up again, their anger turned to relief. They'd fall right back into being a family again whenever Marshall visited. As much as Marshall Senior wanted to pry into Marshall Junior's lifestyle, he didn't.

As the years went on, the visits decreased. What once had happened a couple of times a month became once every three or four months. The same warm greeting from Marshall Senior and Alice would manifest. Their son was alive; this was what mattered most to them. They reluctantly accepted the life Marshall had chosen to lead. They weren't proud of their son, but they felt helpless. Their overwhelming feeling was that they had failed as parents—though they had no idea how or why. Marshall was their only child. They loved him and gave him everything they were able to—material support, their affection, and also their prayers. Marshall's parents prayed every day for their son to turn his life around, and at one point it seemed that their prayers had been answered. When Marshall was twenty-seven, he broke free from the criminal world. He came home, and it seemed that he was going to stay. However, this new chapter in the family's life was short-lived.

The Marshall who returned home at twenty-seven was not the same Marshall who had left in his teens. The once enterprising young man had become reserved and depressed. He was scarred inside himself by the life he'd led. His father and mother attempted to comfort their son and even to pry information from him. They felt it was healthy for him to talk about what was bothering him—certainly better than keeping it bottled up inside. These attempts were not successful, however. Marshall now spent most of his time sitting alone in his bedroom and sinking deeper into depression. He refused to talk with his parents or to see a doctor or a counselor.

After about three months of this reclusive existence, Marshall began making a few trips out of the house. His parents didn't know where he went on these trips. They couldn't stop him from going—hovering over him wasn't the answer—and when he came back, they were delighted.

It happened at a Sunday dinner. These dinners were the only normalcy the family had experienced since Marshall's return. Earlier that day Marshall had left, and he had been gone a bit longer than usual. He arrived just as dinner was being served. Marshall Senior led the dinnertime prayer, and those peaceful words were the last he would ever speak. Under the table his son was holding a loaded .38 caliber revolver. His father was seated to his left. Following the prayer, Marshall, a lefty, raised his hand with the .38 and fired two shots into his father's face. Alice sat in shock as blood from her husband of thirty years spattered across her face. Then Marshall leaned across the table and fired another two bullets into his mother. He pushed his chair out and walked around the corner of the table to get a good look at his dead parents on the floor.

Marshall had seen the dead before. Some were people he had killed, and some were not. He was a professional killer who had never spent a day in jail. I suppose you could say he was good at his trade. But this particular trade carries tremendous guilt and pain, and the pain had reached a level that Marshall could no longer contain. Standing over his parents' bodies, he raised the gun to his temple and, with another flick of the trigger, ended his own life.

While there were similarities between the life experiences of Monty and Marshall, there was at least one key difference. Yes, they had both taken their own lives, but Monty had witnessed his parents' murder while Marshall had murdered his parents himself. Still, Monty took a special interest in Marshall then and continued to do so. Monty explained that he lost Marshall to PopCon and that this loss galled him to this day.

"I could have done more to help him," Monty said. "Just like I could have done more to help my parents."

This was an emotional side of Monty that I hadn't seen much of. I asked him, "How much control do you really think we have when we're alive?"

"Very little," he admitted. Then he said it again with emphasis: "*Very* little. I've learned that here. PopCon can do what they want, and they do it when they want. I realize I'm only one person to their army, but if I can save a soul or—better yet—save someone still alive, I'm going to do everything in my power to do it." I saw tears on his cheeks, but he brushed them away so brusquely that I had to wonder if I'd imagined them.

"What happens if you don't save me?"

"Don't worry, sweet girl. Monty's gotcha." He gave me another wink, and then it was time for us to take the next steps forward in this bizarre adventure.

CHAPTER EIGHT

The banks of the riverbed were mostly rocky without much greenery pushing through. Monty started walking north, and I followed. He wasn't much for conversation when he was walking. I had learned to follow him closely and to honor his preference for silence. I don't believe he avoided conversation purposely; he was just laser-focused on the next task. When Monty passed, he was younger than me. Still, it didn't feel as if I were the elder of the two of us. This may have been due to our appearances. I looked like a teenage girl, while he had the appearance of a crusty guy in his fifties. If our roles had been reversed, it may have been difficult, or maybe impossible, for us not to continually butt heads. We were both stubborn A-type personalities. I have never liked following, and I did it now just to keep the peace. Plus—as Monty had pointed out to me—he was the one with the experience and knowledge. All I had to guide me was my instincts. So far, we hadn't been anywhere that Monty hadn't been. I'd be foolish to not follow his lead. He had my complete trust and confidence. We had known each other only a short time, but I'd learned to trust him. I saw what happened with Joanna, and I didn't want to fall into that trap again. It's possible that, like Joanna, Monty was sinister in his dealings with me, but my gut told me that he wasn't.

Up ahead, the river began to wind slightly to the northwest, and, for the first time, we began to lose our clear view. With each step we took, the flowing water became louder. When we arrived at the point where the river shifted directions, we stepped onto a bed of grass that was about twenty feet in diameter. The soft ground beneath our feet was vibrating slightly, and the grass was approximately ankle high. I noticed that the reason for the sudden increase in the river's sound was a small waterfall that broke just as the river curved. The water took a drop of about ten feet. It was a lovely sight, and there was a fragrance as well.

"What is that?" I said, inhaling deeply through my nose.

"What's what?"

"That wonderful smell."

Monty smiled. "I think that might be the grass we're standing on."

"That's what it is," I said. "Grass. It brings back wonderful memories for me." I dropped to my knees and moved my hands from side to side, bringing them up, one at a time, so that I could get a better whiff of this sweet scent. It was ryegrass, which is what we'd had in our yard in Franklin. We spent a lot of time in our yard as a family, especially when the kids were still crawling. Cliff and I would roll around with them, not minding at all the grass stains that we'd accumulate on our pant knees. Having four kids made for a well-planned hand-me-down system. As much as I worked to remove the grass stains from the onesies, there would always be remnants. As soon as a new crawler entered our lives, out came the old grass-stained onesies. The system worked well until Reese came along. The poor thing had nothing but baby boy clothes to wear.

Monty looked on as I reminisced, giving me my time. "Who was your favorite?" he asked, giving voice to the question most parents would never answer honestly.

"Reese," I said. I was being honest—but only because I was here. I never would have admitted that when I was alive.

"Of course," Monty said with a laugh. "The girl!"

"That has something to do with it, but not everything. Look, I adored my boys, but Reese was the sweetest little girl I'd ever encountered. Such a selfless human being at such a young age." I stopped. Referring to my daughter in the past tense was rattling me. Realizing that she would never grow up tore me up inside.

"I'm sorry, dear," Monty said, putting his arm around me. "I didn't mean to stir up bad memories." It was the first time he'd done anything like that. I looked up at him to see his young eyes staring back. As I had with Joanna, I could see that the eyes tell everything. Had it always been that way, or was it just here?

Monty dropped his arm then and stepped forward to take a peek down to the bottom of the ten-foot drop.

"Where do we go from here?" I asked.

"It's not 'we,'" Monty said. "It's just you now. I can't go past this spot." He pointed at the grass I'd been admiring so much.

Feeling a tremor of fear, I walked over to where Monty was standing. Plummeting down the waterfall, the river picked up speed; it was much faster than before.

"Don't worry," Monty said. "This time you won't be jumping. Look over there." He pointed to the west, where I could now see a path winding down to the hill.

"So, this is it then, right?" I had done whatever I could to distract myself from thinking about what might happen when I reached this particular point—the entryway to Hell. I had conflicting thoughts. Part of me felt that I deserved to go to Hell. But I also felt that I deserved to be with my children—and for that I needed to get to Heaven.

"This is it," Monty agreed. "I'll do my best to stay right here, but I can't guarantee you'll find me." Obviously, he knew this from experience.

I grabbed Monty by the hands and looked him straight in the eyes. "If I don't see you again, please know how much your help and guidance has meant to me. I don't know where I'd be without it." I paused. "I have one more favor to ask."

"Stop," Monty said. And then he answered my question before I could ask it. "I know what to do," he said, "and you can bet that I'll be on the lookout for them. I feel good about where they are. You should feel good about it too.

And that was it: I now knew he would keep an eye out for my children. I turned toward the path.

"Hey, don't worry," Monty said. "I'll see you again." And again, there was the wink.

I took a deep breath and stepped onto the beginning of the steep path Monty had pointed me toward. The way was muddy, and there were some sharp rocks. I figured the rocks would serve as makeshift steps to help me avoid sliding down the path. I placed my right foot on the first rock and sat down in the mud, grabbing whatever I could on either side of me to brace myself. The first rock felt steady under my foot, and my left foot continued on to the next rock. The third rock was farther away, and to get there I'd need to make a small leap, and to trust gravity to do the rest. I counted to three in my head and jumped. My foot found the rock, but I lost my balance—and I fell down the remaining eight feet of the path. I felt pressure on the side of my head, and when my tumble came to an end, everything went black.

It's impossible for me to tell how long I lay in the mud at the bottom of the path, but when I awoke, all was silent. The crashing of the water was gone. The sky above was blue with only a couple of clouds. I tried to turn my head to the left, but I felt a lot of pain on that side of my head. I turned to the right, trying to see the direction I had toppled from. The silence was inexplicable.

When I finally could swivel myself around, I saw that the river had dried up. There was no waterfall—no water at all and no sign that water had ever been there. I gathered myself and made it to my feet, still dizzy from the blow to my head. I ran my fingers through my hair. I found a large knot on my scalp but, surprisingly, no blood. My instincts told me to climb back up the path to find Monty. However, it turned out that backtracking was not an option. The path I'd fallen down no longer had rocks or any other way to scale it. The only move possible was to go forward into the dry riverbed. Following the riverbed down was not an option either. I was blocked in with one choice. I had to cross the riverbed.

The width of this riverbed was at least three hundred yards. Three hundred yards of the unknown. And I didn't know whether my goal was to get across or whether that was just the first step in my journey. I also didn't know what was waiting for me on the other side of this once-riverbed. What was clear is that I'd been given an invitation to cross. So, that's what I needed to do.

Here in the afterlife, it had become all too common for me to take a step forward without the confidence of knowing I would be safe or knowing what was coming next. The painful step I took while holding onto Phonso's hands had been burned into my brain. That incident once again replayed in my head in slow motion. The pain in his eyes told the entire story. He was just a pawn for me to play with. Now, as I took these steps, I was waiting to learn my fate. I have to think that I'd be judged for what I've done on Earth and also for what I've done here.

The riverbed was oddly warm, almost hot, as my feet crunched over it. The only sounds I could hear were the crunching of my feet and my heavy breathing. I was walking cautiously but with no issues. At about fifty yards in, I paused to see if I could locate Monty on the grass above.

No luck. Slowly, I went another fifty yards. At this point, both shores looked a long way away. I went another fifty yards—meaning I was about midway. To the south a breeze began to push through, but still there was no sound. Unfortunately, that wouldn't last.

From a distance, I began to hear water. It was getting louder and louder. I knew exactly what was happening. I began to run to the opposite shore. From my right, water began to flow over the drop. I could see that I wasn't going to make it to the shore. The sound of the water became deafening, much louder than before. I turned my back to the rushing water, knowing that my best bet was to go down the river feet first. I braced myself for the impact, hoping it wouldn't launch me face first into the bottom of the riverbed.

I clenched my fists and leaned back as far as I could without losing my balance. The noise of the water suddenly ended. I was still standing; there had been no impact. I turned around and looked behind me—to the horror of a wall of water at least a hundred feet high and spanning the width of the river. It was as if someone pushed a "pause" button to stop this fierce onslaught of water from attacking me. The sight was eerily similar to the view I had seen from beneath the Memory Pool. The only thing that was missing was the image of the souls fighting their way through it. While this wall wasn't transparent, it wasn't completely opaque either. I could see a little through the water.

A figure began to become visible, moving closer to me but not yet emerging through the wall. Whoever this was, he or she was holding their arms close to their side. When the figure finally became visible—having arrived at a stopping point just short of merging into my space—I saw to my horror that it was my oldest son, Benjamin. For a moment I panicked, wondering if he was now dead as well. Then he emerged from the wall.

Ben was wearing his favorite University of Tennessee T-shirt, orange with a large white T on the front. His Tennessee hat was pulled down low on his forehead and the brim was curled. He was also wearing blue cargo shorts and flip flops—an outfit he wore often.

"Ben, are you OK?" I asked him. Then I asked, "Why are you here?" I hoped the answer wouldn't reveal he was dead.

"I was sent with a message," he said, speaking in an eerie monotone that sounded nothing like him. He looked right through me.

I tried to take a step forward to get closer to him, but I was unable

69

to move. "Ben, look at me. Please tell me what's going on!"

"I told you, I'm here with a message." Again, he responded with no emotion.

"Well, tell me, what are you here for? You're scaring me, Ben."

Ben looked down to the ground, closing his eyes. He lifted his head back up to reveal eyes that were one hundred percent dilated. They were completely black. This couldn't be Ben.

"Ben, is that you? Tell me!"

An emotionless creature that looked like Ben responded, "You will go to Population Control and turn yourself in. You hold vital information that they must receive. If you do not go to Population Control, Ben will die, and Hell will await your arrival. Find Marshall. He will take you there."

After delivering that disheartening message, the figure masquerading as Ben stepped backward and disappeared into the wall of water.

The ground started to rumble as this water wall began to produce waves. My feet were no longer stuck to the riverbed. I started to run as the rumbling increased, the ground shaking furiously below my feet with each step. I chose to run to the north, knowing Population Control was in the opposite direction. I hadn't seen the north section yet and still didn't know what was waiting for me there, but I now knew what was to the west, east, and south. I needed to find out what was to the north, and hopefully I would find Monty in the process.

The water from the wall began spraying along my path, and I knew that the wall would break soon, leaving me to take my chances in the soon-to-be raging river. The bank was twenty yards away… ten yards away… five, four, three yards away, and then I jumped onto the solid, safe land. I hit the ground hard on my chest, and my face slammed to the sandy shale. I heard the sound of the water crashing just a few feet behind me with relief. I knew that I'd made it across the riverbed just in time. I rolled over so I could watch the water crash onto the riverbed, quickly turning it from a dried out barren mess to a rapidly flowing river. The side from which I had come now looked miles away. If I was being watched—and I felt certain that I was—they weren't pleased that I had gone north.

I was rattled and rightfully so. Once again, I would be wandering alone into the unknown—and the landscape to the north wasn't going to be easy to navigate. It was heavily wooded, not at all like the wide-open track to the east. This trek was likely to be much more challenging. I started walking and found that the woods grew thicker as I went into them. The sparsely spaced trees I encountered at first became increasingly abundant. When I came to a small stand of pines, I decided it was time for me to take a little rest. These mental breaks, I had found, made a huge difference. The stress of this world was more than I could handle, yet I didn't have a choice. My head still hurt from my fall, and that was nothing compared to the pressure I felt in this situation where I was just walking into the unknown.

Seeing Ben—or, anyway, seeing someone who appeared to be Ben—and listening to what he demanded had left me, once again, with more questions than answers. It's not that I was afraid of going to Population Control. I knew it had to be done if I was going to arrive at my final goal, which was Heaven. I had been hoping that my trip east would provide me with more self-confidence, that it would give me a "pass" on Hell. I was elated to have survived my first encounter, but hearing that I had to engage with this Marshall was… Well, as I said, it was disheartening. I had been disturbed by Monty's story about Marshall, who was clearly a sick individual and was still wreaking havoc. Why hadn't Marshall gone to Hell? Perhaps when I'd been here a bit longer, I would begin to understand the hierarchy. In this moment, it looked to me as if Population Control ruled this place in much the way Monty implied. It also seemed that God was non-existent, and that this power vacuum had inspired Monty—and probably others like him—to take on battles where he was outnumbered. Somehow, Monty had survived the onslaught and, even though his victories may appear to be small, he had made a difference. He'd made a difference with me already, and I wasn't done yet.

To take my mental breaks, I'd learned to fall deep into meditation. Since I couldn't actually sleep, this was my best option. Just like Monty had lost count of almost everything but the six souls with three-plus vultures, I'd lost count of how many times I had sat in meditation. Each time I'd practice this, my thoughts would run deeper and quieter, and I'd rise with greater energy than before. I'd been getting stronger, and this, in itself, was intoxicating. I was still scared, but my stance had become fearless. That may sound contradictory, but it isn't. I was scared—I was very wary about what might happen—but this didn't in any way stop me from pressing forward. I even moved forward with confidence. It was like having the lead role in a play and having butterflies in my stomach before going on stage. The butterflies were just an acknowledgment of the reality of the situation—which I knew I would be able to face. I was scared, and I knew that I could do this.

I sat underneath the tallest pine tree in the cluster, resting my back against the tree and picking up a handful of pine needles. I raised the needles to eye level and then released them, so they dropped onto my thighs and scattered. I found this simple act to be soothing. When I was growing up, we'd had pine trees bordering our property. As a child, I'd sit underneath the pines and drop handfuls of needles until my lap was covered. I suppose this was my way of escaping. No child should ever feel a need to escape, but, unfortunately, I did. I thought Cliff and I had created a much better home for our children than the one I'd experienced as a child—but I had been wrong about that.

CHAPTER NINE

My tranquil moment ended abruptly. There was rustling behind me, and the sound brought me to my feet. I kept the pine tree between me and the man responsible for the rustling.

Once again, I was being confronted by a man I'd never seen before. I told him, "Stay right there!"

"Maggie, don't be scared," this man said. "I won't hurt you." He knew my name!

The man stood just over six feet tall. He had brown wavy hair, almost shoulder-length, and a thick beard. He appeared to be in his mid-thirties, and his dark brown eyes matched his body's apparent age. His jeans were tattered with holes in the knees, and he wore a mechanic's shirt, minus the usual name. Overall, his appearance was normal except for his shoes. They were boots, but that's not the odd part. The odd part is that he actually had footwear. I stepped back from the pine, and the man closed the gap between us, taking that many steps toward me.

"How do you know my name?" I asked him.

"I asked to come find you," he said. "So, here I am."

"And who did you ask?" Then I told him, "Don't get any closer to me." He looked like a reasonable person, but I knew this counted for very little. My trust needed to be earned.

"Maggie, I understand that you don't recognize me. I don't look anything like I did when we were together." He looked into my eyes—which were the same shade of brown as his.

"No, I don't recognize you."

"I'm your father," he said. "I asked to come here so I could help you. That's my only reason for being here." A smile appeared through his thick beard.

The last time I'd seen my father was when I was ten. I knew Mom had communicated with him on and off over the first five or six years after he'd left. And then that thin line of connection had ended as well. Mom and I hadn't known if Dad was dead or alive and, really, we didn't much care. If he'd been hoping I'd welcome him with open arms, he was sorely mistaken. I wanted to run over and punch him in the face. Seeing Dad right now was almost as bad as running into someone from PopCon or encountering Joanna again. She was someone who had said she wanted to help me—and look what had happened with her!

"I don't want your help," I told him. "Just go back to where you came from." I pointed over his shoulder, assuming that he came from that direction.

"I can't go back without helping you," he said. "They won't let me." There he was again, talking about someone or something being in control of his actions. It was spooky.

"Who won't let you?" I demanded.

"I know you've learned a lot about this place," he said. "I've been watching your path and it's led you here. Before you go to PopCon, you need to come with me." He was almost pleading with me to follow him.

"How do I know you're telling the truth?" I asked him. "I need some proof that you're who you say you are."

"Sure," he said. "But what kind of proof do you want?"

"Tell me something that only my father would know, and then I'll decide whether or not I'm going to follow you."

"There's a scar on your ankle," he said. "I know how you got it, and I'm not proud of it."

That was all I needed to hear. This man was my father. My memories of my father were violent. His violence was directed primarily at my mother, but I would occasionally be his target. My scar was proof of that. As much as I'd like to, I'll never forget that night. It was the last time in my life that I'd seen my father.

It was October 30th, a Thursday night and the eve of what had been my favorite holiday, Halloween. I'd always enjoyed dressing up and pretending to be something I wasn't—even though it was only for one day. This was something I looked forward to all year long. I'd plan my costume months in advance, and sometimes I knew what my next Halloween costume would be a full year ahead. At the time, I was fascinated with the film *The Wizard of Oz* and while Dorothy may have been the popular choice, I chose Glenda, the good witch. I loved everything about Glinda. She was beautiful and caring and adored by the Munchkins, and she had Dorothy's best interests at heart. It was Glinda who told her how she could go home. I had always loved Glinda—and even now, in the afterlife, I found myself wishing I'd stumble across a Glinda of my own.

My father had been disinterested in Halloween or, for that matter, in anything else that had to do with the family. My brother Martin was six that year, and he dressed as a baseball player, a New York Yankees baseball player to be precise. It was a bit of a cop-out since the Little League team he had played for earlier that year was the Yankees. Martin just wore a Little League uniform, cleats and all. I was disappointed in him, and so was Mom. We'd had plenty of other ideas for Martin, but his stubbornness won.

Mom and I were putting the final touches on my Glinda costume when my father walked in. He was early, and he was drunk. His target, as usual, was Mom. For some reason he hated her, and for some reason she put up with it. I was standing on the family room ottoman, and Mom was hemming the bottom of my dress to make sure I wouldn't trip over it while I was going house to house. My father walked over to us, spewing profanities. One thing I caught was "How much did this fucking thing cost?" Mom's chosen method of dealing with him was to ignore him, which she did right now. He stepped closer and asked his question again. She ignored him again. Finally, he shoved his chest into her, sending her to the ground. I remained standing on the ottoman with my bird's eye view of Mom on the ground and Dad hovering over her. He yelled at her, calling her a bitch, telling her to get up, and grabbing her by the hair. My mom hit him in the face.

I don't remember her ever hitting him before. I got excited when I saw that: Mom was finally going to fight back. My startled father fell down, and Mom ran out the back door and into the yard. My father followed, and I did too, hoping I could help my mother. They were in the middle of the backyard, my father lunging over my mother, swinging at her with a closed fist. Her shrieks pierced my soul. It was a sound I'll never forget. I ran as fast as I could, jumping onto my father's back as he leaned in on my helpless mother. He had blood on both of his fists—her blood! He stood up, grabbing my hands, removing them from around his neck, and throwing me a good ten feet.

I landed awkwardly, feeling a sharp pain in my left ankle and then seeing blood flow freely from the cut. I had landed on a shovel. My father had thrown me with such force that the point of the shovel pierced my ankle, tearing the ligaments. I started screaming then; my mom had just stopped. She rushed over to me and hugged me as the tears ran down my face. The blood was collecting on my dress, and I remember crying as much for my ruined costume as for my deep wound.

Mom held me, and we both stared down at my father. For once, I could see fear in his eyes. His bullying had gone too far. No longer was he just abusing my mom. He had hurt his daughter. Mom demanded that he leave for good. "If you don't," she said, "I'm calling the police." Dad took one more look at us, and he left. That was it. I hadn't seen him since.

Now, I was face-to-face with someone who looked like a stranger to me but was nothing of the sort. I had spent the first ten years of my life with this man. I had watched him wreak havoc around what we attempted to call a family. Martin was lucky. Not only did he barely remember our father, but he had also never been the target of his anger. I was only four years older than Martin, but those four years—and maybe being female—made all the difference in the world. Anger, pain, and abuse were inflicted on me and Mom on a regular basis. It took a while for me to understand the importance of Dad's departure and how it had saved the three of us. I was certain it would all come to a violent end with the life of one of my parents ending. But for some reason he left that night, and now he was here, asking to play a part in my journey to find my own children, his grandchildren. Just looking at him and knowing that he was my father made me fearful.

"I believe you're who you say you are," I said. "So, now tell me how you can help me."

Dad was pacing slowly, looking at the ground. "Before I do that," he said, "I'd like to explain something to you."

"And that is?"

"I wanted to find you not only so I could help you, but also to help relieve you of the burden you're carrying." He looked up, catching my eye. "I know you feel like your children's deaths were in part due to your actions."

I was outraged to hear this. "I find it rude and presumptuous of you to claim to know anything about me," I told him, "anything at all."

He addressed this indirectly. "I've been here longer than you," he said, "and every moment I spend here, I learn more."

"So, what does that make you?"

I wasn't expecting an answer, but he replied immediately and with perfect calm. "It makes me someone who can help you," he said. "And I promise you that's all I want to do. I owe it to you."

I didn't really care about his sense of duty. "I want to be with my children," I said. "I want to get out of here and get to Heaven, so I can be with them. If you can't help me with that, then forget it."

I walked straight toward him but instead of meeting him head-on, I stepped just to his right and went past him, walking in the direction from which he had come. Maybe I was just too proud to accept an offer of assistance from someone who had caused me so much pain. Anyway, I had made it this far without his help, so I decided I would just go.

When I was about twenty yards past him, he said, "You're as stubborn as your mother."

If he had hoped to elicit a strong response from me, he succeeded. I turned around and ran at him like a bull might. After my first few steps it was clear that he wasn't going to budge. I launched myself into the air, planting an elbow on his nose. We both tumbled to the ground as he grabbed his face. He felt the pain, which surprised me. I had been under the impression that physical pain was nonexistent here. Clearly, that wasn't true.

"And as strong as she was, too," he rubbed his nose and wiped away a bit of blood.

"Why are you here?" I asked him again. "You were horrible to me when we were alive, and now you're doing it all over again?"

"I don't have a choice," he said. "I asked to help you, and now I can't go back without having accomplished my task. If I don't do this, they won't take me."

Another reference to "they," which both annoyed me and piqued my curiosity. "I'll listen to what you have to say," I told him, "but at some point I need to know who this 'they' is."

Knowing that I might have opened up a can of worms—and that I might come to regret it—I took a seat on a handy rock and motioned him to a spot on a rock nearby. This son-of-a-bitch had done nothing for me while I was alive, but I could give him his shot at redemption now. I felt as though my every step was leading me one step closer to my kids. If I had to dredge up parts of my past that I'd thought I'd never experience again, then so be it.

"I won't act like you don't remember that night before Halloween," he told me. "But I lived with it every day for the rest of my life, and for every moment after I died." I could hear that the sincerity of these words flowed from his soul.

"I was surprised that you listened to Mom that night," I said. "I saw for the first time that you looked terrified."

"I suppose that was my rock bottom. Seeing you in pain on the ground next to your battered mother was all I could take of my being the way I was. I had become a monster, and the worst kind of monster—the kind that preys on women and children. I wanted to die that night, and, truthfully, I almost did."

"Almost?"

"Yes, I should have died that night, but someone was watching out for me."

My father had left Mom and me and returned to the ratty old bar he frequented, the Iron Keg. He knew all of the guys who were still bellied up at the bar. They were all alcoholics, and some were into drugs as well. One guy in particular, Lenny, had a knack for drumming up nasty cocktails of cocaine, OxyContin, and anything else he thought might provide him with the ultimate high. My father would sometimes smoke a little pot, but usually, he stuck with alcohol. He was fond of straight bourbon. On this night, Lenny was sitting next to him, fidgeting and high as a kite.

"Marty, welcome back, you fucking lush." Lenny said, leaning in on him and stinking of cheap tequila. "I knew you'd be back tonight."

"Get the fuck off of me, man," my father said, pushing Lenny away and sliding over to the empty bar stool on his other side.

"What's the problem, man?" Lenny said, moving himself onto the bar stool my father had vacated. "You need to relax. I can help you with that, man."

Usually, my father would have ignored Lenny and ordered another bourbon. But after his horrible evening, he decided that maybe he should partake. It would be a means to an end—a means to the end.

"OK Lenny, whatcha got for me?"

"Now we're talking. I can give you a taste for free, but for any more than that, I need to see some green." Lenny grabbed my father's shoulder, getting his first good look at the blood on his shirt.

My father pulled out a wad of cash—he'd just been paid in cash for a handyman gig. "I'm covered, Lenny. Now give me what you've got."

"Step into my office." Lenny got up from his stool and motioned for my father to follow him to the restroom.

The Iron Keg was a shithole beyond shitholes. As long as patrons weren't breaking anything and paid their tabs, it was an "anything goes" kind of place. An example of this was the bathroom. The stalls weren't used for defecation. They were private drug stalls.

When they got into the bathroom, the two stalls were locked. "Come on," Lenny yelled, pounding on one stall door. "Get the fuck outta there. Let's go!"

The stall door opened, emptied out another druggie, and welcomed Lenny and my father.

As soon as the door closed, Lenny pulled out a small foil packet. "This is the shit, man. You want to get high? This is the stuff to do it!"

My father's heart raced. He knew what was in the foil.

"Have a seat and I'll get you set up." Lenny pulled out a spoon that appeared to be well-used for moments like this. A syringe followed. "Hold this," Lenny gave my father the syringe and spoon as he pulled his belt off.

My father, whose drug history had only been marijuana, which barely qualifies as a drug, was about to inject heroin into his veins. His intention was simple: he was going to kill himself.

"Put a little more in there. I have the money." My father waved the cash in Lenny's face.

"You're going for it. Alright, my man!" Lenny, scumbag that he was, didn't truly care that he was about to kill my father with a lethal dose of heroin.

Lenny flicked the lighter, and the heroin was cooked. The belt was tightly secured on my father's arm. Lenny did the honors, filling up the syringe and handing it over to my father. The vein in his left arm was bulging and primed for the syringe. The needle was inserted, and a small burst of blood floated into the syringe. He pushed the plunger and felt the immediate rush. The euphoria of the moment didn't last long. The intense rush and tremendous feeling came—and went. It ended with a crash as my father fell to the floor, foaming at the mouth. His plan was almost complete. Lenny ran from the bathroom, leaving my father on the floor to die.

The bartender noticed Lenny running out the bar's front door. Knowing something was wrong, this bartender, Kyle, hurried to the bathroom and found my father, almost lifeless on the filthy floor.

I was both shocked and saddened as I listened to this story. As much as I hated my father, I couldn't help but feel bad for him. I think I've heard more about suicide here in the afterlife than when I was alive. Monty's pain had led to him taking his own life and now my father was sitting here sharing his own suicidal moment. Dad, however, did not succeed in taking his own life.

"I woke up in intensive care about five hours later," he told me. "I had no idea how I'd gotten there." In his blurred vision, he could see a policeman scowling at him, wanting some answers because, of course, he had overdosed and had blood all over his clothes.

"So, you ran from us that night and then tried to run away from your own life." I was shaking my head like a disapproving parent.

"Yep, that's accurate." He didn't seem to care that I was judging him.

"Then what?"

"To my surprise, I wasn't charged with anything, but I met someone that night who would become my savior. That's the night I met Margaret. Yep, Margaret. I don't feel it was a coincidence either." He tried to take my hand then, but I rebuffed him.

"Please don't tell me you fell in love." I said. "I don't have the stomach to hear a happily-ever-after."

"No, no, no." He was chuckling a bit now. "Margaret was assigned to me. She was there to help me. I was an addict, and it was clear I needed help. The next time I did something like this, I'd be dead."

My father picked up his story from the moment he'd met Margaret and proceeded all the way to this moment. Margaret's role at the hospital was to identify those who needed counseling and guidance, not just to turn their lives around but also to save them from themselves. My father was clearly a candidate for a service like this. The only question was whether he would take this help or choose to fall back into the dark hole he had been pulled out of by the hospital staff.

As he'd said, he should have died that night. The doctors, the nurses, and everyone else who was involved saw his survival as a miracle. They were faced with such cases all the time and knew that more than ninety percent of them end in death. The physical body can take only so much, and my father had pushed his to the brink. Still, he had enough strength to survive the lethal dose of heroin that flowed through his body that night.

The police asked questions that are typical in a case like this. They wanted to know who had supplied the heroin and where they could find that person. My father was tight-lipped on the subject, but the police were resourceful. They knew the dealer would be right back at it in the Iron Keg—and sure enough he was. It was just a couple days later when Lenny was arrested. He had a menagerie of drugs and drug paraphernalia on him, making it easy for the authorities to lock him up for a long time. Lenny never admitted to being my father's Dr. Kevorkian, but the police knew he was involved.

"I was in the hospital for the next five days," my father told me. "Margaret visited me every day. She needed to know if I was committed to making the necessary changes in my life."

After his release, he moved into a halfway house with other addicts. My mother had been notified when he'd arrived at the hospital after the overdose, but she chose to stay clear of the drama. Believe it or not, this wasn't easy for her. At one time, she had been madly in love with my father. The monster he'd turned into was too much for her, though, and at this point she was able to quit him cold turkey. She meant what she said when she demanded he leave for good. While she was surprised when he actually listened to her, she was pleased with the result. He was gone.

Living in a halfway house was a sobering experience for my father—in every way. Yes, he stayed away from alcohol and drugs, but also his foggy vision of his life became crystal clear. The mistakes he'd made, the pain he'd caused—all of this kept him awake at nights. His guilt, nightmares, and withdrawals were painful remnants of his past. Like many addicts, he was pulled by the urge to fall off the wagon, to have "just one drink." He'd wake up every morning to the battles and the temptations that day would bring him. He went to AA meetings regularly, picking up his chips when he reached various milestones. Each one was another sign that he was beating his addiction. He worked the steps. He recited his favorite prayer every morning as he got up and every night before he went to sleep. His favorite prayer happened to be the same as mine: The Serenity Prayer.

Years passed, and the urge to drink did not subside. Every year, another chip and a brief feeling of accomplishment. Then the sun would set on that day, and another year would begin. October 30th was always the hardest day of the year for him. On that day, not only was he tempted to drink, but he also had an almost unbearable urge to reach out to my mother to see how she and their children were doing.

Alcoholism was at the forefront of his remaining years on Earth. He got involved in a few relationships, but he pulled away for fear of hurting others like he'd hurt my mom and Martin and me. He ended up following Margaret's lead, becoming a counselor himself. Seeing and helping others face and beat their demons was truly gratifying. Sometimes, of course, he had to watch helplessly as those he was counseling would relapse. That was when he felt the most vulnerable. It was as if every person he attempted to help became a part of him. When someone would relapse, he felt as if he'd relapsed as well. Unfortunately, there were quite a few who lost their battles, succumbing to alcohol, drugs, or the violence that was related to their lifestyle.

In the end, he died without any blood family with him. I can't say that he died alone, though. His family of fellow addicts—both those he counseled and others whom he had come to love because of their common bond—were at his side as he battled cancer. He received a diagnosis of pancreatic cancer, and only five months later he was gone. No one was listed as next of kin, but his funeral was glorious. In the thirty-six years he'd managed to stay clean, he had touched so many lives, helping not only the addicts themselves but also their family members. The church was overflowing with well-wishers when he was laid to rest. My father had successfully channeled the good he had inside him and shared it with those who desperately needed help.

Hearing his life story gave me mixed emotions. I couldn't help but think that I had been robbed of the good that this man had shared with so many. Starting on that October night, I had spent all the rest of the years of my life hating him. Tears were rolling down my cheeks as he finished his story.

"We all have our paths I suppose," he said. "And this was mine." I suspected that he was looking at the same thing I was: missed opportunities.

I'm not sure what my father's goal was in talking with me, but if it had anything to do with gaining my trust, he'd succeeded.

"Where to now?" I was ready to follow him.

"Nathan is waiting for us," he said, throwing out the name of yet another person I was supposed to trust. "He needs to meet you first."

"Let's walk," I said. "And while we walk, I'm sure you'll tell me everything I need to know about Nathan." I was being sarcastic. Still, I was ready to go with my father.

"It's not too far from here," he said, clearly pleased that he had won my trust. "Let's get moving. We can get there before dark."

The walk wasn't pleasant. The once solid ground that we had been walking on turned into a muddy mess. So much so that my father, the only one with footwear, would occasionally get his shoes stuck in the mud. After it happened a couple of times, he took off the shoes and carried them. The abundance of mud wasn't allowing us to make much headway, and I was doubtful that we'd get to wherever we were going before the sun went down.

"There's no way we'll get there at this pace," I said, looking to where the sun continued to dip lower and lower toward the horizon.

"You might be right," he told me, "but don't worry about it. I'll get us there even if it's in the dark." I could see how he ended up being a successful counselor. The confidence in his tone put me at ease.

"So, tell me about Nathan," I said. It was the obvious question.

"You'll like Nathan, trust me. He's a tremendous leader." This answer, which was almost cult-like, had the opposite effect on me than my father had been looking for.

"Just to be clear," I told him, "I'm going to meet with Nathan so he can help me. I hope it's not the other way around." I paused for a second, and then realized I needed more clarification from my father. I said, "I don't know what the hell I'm doing here. The pressure to help others is just too much for me. I am not looking to help Nathan. I am only interested in him helping me."

"It'll all be clear when we get there and you sit with him." My father was clearly trying to put me at ease. "You'll see that it's going to be a mutually beneficial relationship. Trust me."

I didn't have a good feeling about being told to trust someone, but I kept quiet. We continued to trudge through the mess at our feet, finally reaching a clearing that held an unassuming building—the first structure I'd seen since arriving.

"There it is!" My father turned around, met my eyes, and pointed at this building. It was one-story and spread wide to the east and west. A set of double doors split the east and west portions of the building; I couldn't see any windows. It looked like an old warehouse. Still, it piqued my interest. I hadn't expected to come across a structure at all.

"What's in there?"

"You'll see." We followed a concrete path to the double doors.

CHAPTER TEN

The steel double doors contained no mechanism to open them—no doorknob, handle, or latch. Both doors were painted a deep red except for a twelve-by-twelve inch square in a faded shade of the red—maybe a rose—that was about chest high. My father placed the full palm of his right hand on the faded square, his fingers spread, and with his other hand, he caught hold of my hand. I felt a coolness run through my body as the faded square began to emit light all around my father's palm. A burst of cold air engulfed me, and we were transported inside. I felt a change, but wasn't sure what it was. I looked at my hands and noticed that I suddenly had fingernail polish on. The color was a light orange. Seeing this gave me chills. This was the color I had painted my nails on the day I was murdered. I had never worn the shade before, so its connection to that fateful day was clear.

"What's happening?" I asked, putting my hands down so I didn't have to look at the color again.

"It's OK. Don't worry. We're safe in here." My father turned and looked me in the eye as he spoke, obviously attempting to calm me down.

Looking at him, I felt my heart sink. The face looking at me was the same face that had left us on that fateful October night. The trust he had built began to erode. I was seeing the man who had hurt me so badly that night—a monster!

"I can't do this!" I turned back to the door, but now there was no way out. The door was gone.

"What's wrong, Maggie? What is it?" My father caught hold of my shoulder and spun me around.

"Don't touch me!" I could see that I was at the mercy of this man.

"Maggie!" A deep voice startled us both. It was Nathan.

The man stepped toward the two of us, moving slowly. Although he was quite tall—about six-seven—his lanky body didn't convey a sense of fear. His dark blonde hair was almost shoulder length with a bit of a wave to it. The stubble on his face revealed some gray hairs, which seemed odd because he looked as if he were in his early thirties.

I decided to examine his eyes as I'd learned the eyes reveal the true age. His eyes were quite striking, an interesting shade of green, and seemed to belong to a guy in his thirties.

"I'm glad you made it," Nathan said, offering his hand.

"Why am I here?" I asked, accepting that hand.

"We'll figure that out together. But I can assure you that you're here for a reason—an important reason. I have my theories. Let's have a seat, and we can talk about them," Nathan motioned ahead to a long hallway in front of us.

It was quite a sterile environment, almost hospital-like. The floor didn't have a speck of dirt on it. My father and I had been miraculously cleansed of any mud that may have tagged along from our walk there. Just entering the door, we had been transformed. Not only were my fingernails the same shade as they'd been on the day I died, my entire outfit was the same. No mirror was available, but I placed my hand just below my jaw on the right side of my face. I had a small scar there that had happened when I was thirty-eight. Sure enough, I felt the scar leading me to believe that my teenage appearance was gone. I was now the woman from that fateful night. And my father was the man from the other most fateful night in my life. We both followed Nathan.

Nathan led the way, his shoes clicking on the floor as he walked. He was wearing black dress shoes, black pants, and a white long-sleeved dress shirt with no pockets. A skinny black tie was barely long enough, falling about an inch shy of his waistline. I was the only one not wearing anything on my feet, and the floor was freezing. It was beyond cold; it felt frozen, though it wasn't icy. My father walked beside me. I kept my eyes focused on Nathan; I still felt funny looking at the version of my father who had done all those awful things on that night. I didn't want to feel that way, but I didn't know how to feel any different. I wished he would go back to the way he'd looked before we came here. Having heard and understood his story, I had started to feel close to that version of him. I wanted to forgive him. Growing up without a father had been painful. It made me think of Ben. Ben would live the rest of his days without either mother or father—especially since Cliff might receive the death penalty before this was all over. I had mixed feelings about that, but I couldn't quite put a finger on why that was.

A door at the end of the hallway was slightly ajar. We passed several other doors on either side of the hallway, each looking similar to the door on the outside of this building. No handles, knobs, or latches were to be seen. I was tempted to place my palm on one of the squares to see what might happen, but I knew that I'd probably best leave these doors unopened. I might find something I don't want any part of.

When Nathan arrived at the final doorway, he turned to us. "Martin, I'll take it from here," Nathan addressed my father formally.

"Wait a second. I'm not going without you!" I turned to my father, pleading with him.

"I can't, Maggie. This is your time, not mine. I'm sorry." He began walking back down the long hallway.

"Will I see you again?" I asked.

"Of course, you will!" He turned his head and smiled at me, giving me a wink.

Still, I had my doubts that I'd see him again. I felt like I knew so much about him, but he knew nothing about me and my family. I wanted to share that with him. His grandchildren were such special kids. Referring to them in the past tense was unsettling, and it angered me. The worst moments for me here were those when I'd been able to reflect on what had happened. The distractions had been plentiful, but on occasion I'd had moments of clarity when it all came back. The realization that my children had died was bad enough, but to know that it happened in such a horrific manner made me doubt the presence of God—or, at the very least, doubt his power.

But then, the more I'd learned about Population Control, the less I blamed God. It appeared that God's power to rid our world of evil was minimal. His role is to create life, not end it. His creations, my children, were a gift. Gifts that were taken away from me. Whether I was partially responsible or not, it didn't change the fact that they had been ripped away from me. It was all unfair. While I knew I'd accomplish nothing by throwing myself a pity party, I felt I had every right to be sad. The ups and downs I'd been experiencing would continue, I figured, until we were reunited. This is why I was open to walking through this door with

Nathan. I had to believe he could help me. The ability to believe—believe in the good—was all I had right now.

"Follow me, Maggie," Nathan used the palm of his right hand to fully open the door.

I followed, entering a room that was about a fifty-foot square. In the center sat an oval table with four chairs, two on either side of the oval. Why four? It made me wonder if someone else might be joining us.

"This is your chair, Maggie. Please have a seat." Nathan pulled a chair out for me, and I settled in, facing the farthest wall from us.

"Now, let's get down to business." Nathan slid into the chair beside me—a chair that looked not quite big enough for his lanky frame.

"What am I supposed to do here?" I asked him. My purpose had yet to be defined.

Nathan smiled and turned his chair toward mine. "I said before that I had my theories. Let me share them with you to see if you can piece anything together from what I say."

Nathan began to share his knowledge with me, hoping to figure out why I'd arrived and to whose advantage it might be to take me under their wing. It turned out that he was the leader of a small group that controls the souls moving from life to afterlife and vice versa. When I say small, I mean small. While PopCon has souls that number in the hundreds of thousands, the Gateway has fewer than a hundred. Nathan said he didn't believe that power comes in numbers. That was either an optimistic outlook or it was factual. Nathan, of course, believed it to be fact.

The mind didn't die when it joined the Gateway, whereas in PopCon the mind was altered to rid it of all original thought. Those souls were transformed into nothing more than a machine, robbing them of their afterlives. Once they were rejected at Heaven's gate, their journey back down the path brought them to PopCon, where they were put to work monitoring lives on Earth and, more importantly, destroying lives. I had been rejected, but I didn't end up at PopCon, and that was why Nathan had fought hard to get me here, using my father to fetch me from the unknown that existed outside this building.

On occasion Nathan would ask me questions about my journey to date. He took in every word I shared, apparently logging them into his memory. After I'd rambled on with detail after detail, I paused for a moment.

"Are you recording this?" I asked him. "I see you're not writing anything down."

"With something as important as this, there's no chance I'll forget any detail, even the smallest—like the insults to your dress at the sweet sixteen party. Yep, Mark Benson. I'll let you know if he wanders into our lives here someday." Nathan drew a smile from me—and drove home his point at the same time.

"How many times have you come across people like me?" I asked him. "People who have traveled as much as I have but haven't found their final resting place." I wondered if my situation was unique.

"Let me put it this way," he said. "If this were an archaeological dig, you'd be the equivalent of finding every bone of a Tyrannosaurus Rex. Rare." Once again, he smiled.

"Is that why your group is so small?"

"Yes and no. We're not a normal destination. See, not everyone even gets caught here. The majority of souls go right to Heaven or Hell directly. We only get what I liked to call 'the tweeners.'"

"Why does PopCon have so many?"

"You know the answer to that. You just experienced it. It's that damn pathway. They take advantage of these souls when they're at their lowest. Think about how you felt when you saw your kids at the gate but couldn't get in. Horrible, right?"

"Wow, now I'm starting to understand how lucky I was to get by them. But it doesn't explain why they didn't try harder to bring me to PopCon."

"And there you have it, my dear! That's why you're here. That's what we need to figure out."

So, this was my importance to him and the rest of the Gateway.

Nathan had only scratched the surface with his theories. He continued to enlighten me, not holding back any details, which gave me confidence that he was placing trust in me. And I reciprocated. We went back and forth. He'd ask me questions, and I'd return with questions of my own. As much as we began to piece things together, we both agreed that we were trying to complete a puzzle without having all of the pieces. We needed to fill the gaps somehow, and this would require me to venture back out to Vulture Point with an eventual trip to PopCon.

Nathan shared with me what he knew about PopCon's leadership structure. Much like Gateway, PopCon had one leader they followed. There was evidently one primary difference in the leadership styles in the two groups. Nathan led by soliciting feedback from those who followed him, while PopCon was ruled like a dictatorship. Their leader, Cain, was coming to the end of his reign. Nathan said he didn't know how long Cain had been in power, but he seemed certain the end was near. Cain was not the name he had been given at birth; he had adopted the name when he began his rule.

There had been six leaders before Cain. His tenure had been the most violent ever, and his final act was going to be choosing his successor. Cain had challenged the process, attempting to continue his reign beyond the customary time, but this ploy had failed. This appeared to be the one and only thing that was out of Cain's control. Nathan explained that the soul—any soul—eventually becomes depleted, leading to its non-existence. This is what would happen to Cain when his rule ended. He would simply vanish. PopCon knew the exact time when this would happen and was preparing to move forward under new rule. The only threat to PopCon was Nathan's Gateway.

Nathan told me that the competition between these two groups was not at all like warfare on Earth. Here, the power of the mind and the soul ruled all outcomes. This is why Nathan was not concerned with being outnumbered. The minds of most of the souls in PopCon had been drained; they were just not a threat. Cain had a small group of powerful lieutenants who assisted him, but that group is about the same size as Gateway. Therefore, the playing field was fairly even.

"Don't take this wrong," Nathan told me, "but we need to milk you of all your knowledge." Nathan got up from his chair and began to pace. "I know that sounds horrible," he added, "but I think you hold the key."

"Please don't put all your eggs in my basket," I said. "I don't want to disappoint you." The pressure of this situation was starting to get to me. "You make it sound like I'm some kind of chosen one, but that makes no sense to me. My life was as normal as it gets. Quite boring actually. And I didn't make wonderful choices there at the end."

"You have nothing to lose. You'll eventually find your own definition of peace whether you help us or not. Anyway," he added, "you arrived here for a reason, and it would be irresponsible of me to ignore this opportunity to challenge PopCon. They're vulnerable right now. This is our chance. Will you help us?"

Nathan was leaning on the table, his hands palm down. His formerly confident demeanor had begun to seem a little desperate. I looked deep into his light blue eyes, searching for my answer. The eyes didn't lie here. These deep stares haven't steered me wrong yet. I'd been learning whom to trust, and it seemed as if Nathan was definitely on my side.

"Yes, let's do this." I rose from my chair as Nathan walked around to my side of the table. We shook hands as if we had just closed a business deal.

I'd always been a competitive person. When I was young, gymnastics was my sport. I wasn't Olympic caliber, but then again, how many people are? I was quite good though. I earned a college scholarship to University of Georgia, and I won several competitions during my four years there, including the National Championship on the balance beam. Nathan's description of Gateway's role in this crazy world had gotten my competitive juices flowing again. I enjoyed the feeling that I had a purpose here, a defined role. This helped serve as a distraction to my primary interest of reuniting with my children.

Nathan explained our plan of attack, breaking it into three parts. The first was to gather knowledge and information. The next was to take that knowledge into the field to gain support for our mission and build numbers. The final phase was to overthrow PopCon. Yes, his plan was to overthrow PopCon.

"We have to put an end to their rule, Maggie."

"Can that be done?" I knew they had been in power for such a long time.

"Of course, it can. More importantly, it has to happen. We cannot fail."

"And, if we are victorious?" I needed to know what rewards were going to come at the end of this battle.

"If we win, we save all souls," Nathan said, "but more importantly, we save all future souls. Those trapped by PopCon now will be free. The souls who have yet to arrive, the living, will get what they've been promised. They will receive an afterlife free of pain, free of strife. It will be filled with love; they will be surrounded by family and friends." So, Nathan's goals were lofty and selfless.

"How is PopCon hurting the living?" I asked. Ben was my first thought; I didn't want his path to Heaven to be impeded by anyone.

"They hurt the living every minute of every day," Nathan said, his voice rising. "Cain's goal is to put an end to the living altogether, and his time is running out. That's why our time is now!"

Nathan positioned himself at the end of the table and started providing me with information—ammunition—he had on PopCon and Cain. When PopCon had first come into power its role was fairly simple. Just as the name indicates PopCon was in charge of controlling the population. This was a vital function, necessary for the survival of life on Earth. The planet could support only so many inhabitants. Contrary to speculation about life existing on other planets and in other universes, it seems that only the planet Earth contains living beings. There are absolutely no other living forms in existence anywhere else.

Nathan said that Earth is the ninth planet to have supported life and that now it is the only planet to do so. The other eight planets were in different galaxies. Their names were Solan (which had been the first), Gothar, Erronimus, Kaplar, Ferrot Ceren, Poligma, Vice, and (most recently) Santor Hex. Over the course of millions of years, all of the other planets that could sustain life came to an end. Solan and Gothar had ended peacefully—sadly, of course, but peacefully. On those two planets, the living beings simply became extinct. On all the rest of the planets—Erronimus through Santor Hex—the endings were violent. It's no coincidence that Erronimus was the first to end under the rule of PopCon. The violence had escalated with every planet afterwards, all ending with pain and horror impacting the living and the dead as they watched their loved ones perish, never to be reunited in Heaven.

Solan and Gothar ended due to natural causes, much like a candle burning out; life simply disappeared. Both planets still exist but are inhabitable. Erronimus, on the other hand, was the first planet to be destroyed along with every being on it. In the time since, PopCon had not only escalated the violence, but they'd also shortened the lifespan of each successive planet. Nathan said he was not a hundred percent sure, but he believed that the destruction of each planet had taken place at the end of a ruler's term. Since Cain's term was about to end, Earth's existence was about to end as well.

"So, Cain has three goals to accomplish before his rule ends," Nathan said. "Destroy Earth, find a successor, and create the next inhabitable planet."

Nathan let that sink in for a moment before adding, "Earth shouldn't have to end violently. If we can stop Cain, then we'll be able to place his successor and lead the world to the proper end for Earth. We would be saving millions of souls in the process!"

It still wasn't clear to me just how we were going to accomplish any of this, but Nathan evidently felt he had the answers. The door behind me opened. I swiveled around in my chair to see who had entered. It was an old man, and he didn't look familiar to me. He moved slowly, but without assistance. His straight gray hair was slicked back behind large ears. His nose was bulbous, the kind of nose that usually indicates an alcoholic. He was hunched over a bit as he caught hold of the table and took one of the chairs across from me.

"I believe we're ready," Nathan said, walking over to the older gentleman. "Maggie, meet Nigel; Nigel, meet Maggie." Nathan was standing beside the table now, between the two of us.

Nigel said to me, "So, you're the one we've been waiting for?" His voice didn't match his appearance. A forty-year-old voice coming out of a ninety-year-old body.

I must have looked surprised, because Nigel changed his voice then, as if he were impersonating an old man. "Is this better?" he asked me. When I nodded, he laughed.

Nathan spoke up then. "Remember when I said our knowledge and brains would prevail in this fight? Well, you're looking knowledge in the face. Nigel goes way back."

It turned out that Nigel had been an inhabitant of Gothar, the last planet whose ending had been peaceful. He had witnessed PopCon's takeover soon after and had watched them destroy every planet in their path since.

He said, "You see, those PopCon mother fuckers are evil, but you—yes you, Maggie—can stop them. I'm quite certain that you've been sent to us for a reason and, to be blunt, that reason is to save the world."

"All of your loved ones are counting on you," Nathan chimed in.

The weight of my task was beginning to sink in. Ben was in danger as well as everyone else I loved who was still alive—and that included Cliff. Yes, I still loved Cliff. I guess hate hadn't taken over, since I felt that I was just as guilty as Cliff for what had happened that fateful night. It was very difficult to understand, but I could see that hating Cliff didn't do anything positive for me. I needed to remove hatred from my being as it was quite clear I had much bigger enemies to face. I'd been learning about Cain and PopCon, but I couldn't see a compelling reason to hate them either. I feared PopCon, but I had yet to develop hatred for them.

"Nigel, look at me." I grabbed his wrist and looked intently into his eyes. He obliged me by looking back.

To my surprise, I saw that Nigel's right eye was covered with film much like cataracts. His other eye was brown and crystal clear. He looked at me with his good eye and took a deep breath. He knew what I was doing and was comfortable with it. I eased up on his wrist, and he winked at me. We were on the same team.

"Now that I've passed the test," Nigel said, "let's get moving." We both smiled. We were developing a rapport.

I asked, "What do you need me to do?"

"A little bit of soul jumping."

"Excuse me?" I was thinking, *Soul jumping? What the hell is that? And what does a little bit mean?*

"Yep, we need information, and that's what it will take. Right now, you're tapped out, and we're tapped out. We need to mine the information we need from other souls," Nigel motioned to a doorway on the side of the room—a door I hadn't been through before.

Nathan said, "Don't worry, Maggie. We've done this before. You're not a guinea pig."

"But what does it mean?"

Nigel then explained the process of soul jumping. "We refer to ourselves as the Gateway, right? That there is a gateway to Heaven or Hell is obvious, but the most important gateway for us is the path back to the living souls left behind on Earth." Nigel's blind eye twitched slightly as he continued his explanation.

"You're going to jump into Ben's soul," Nathan said.

"What?" I was shocked—and frightened at the thought.

"Yep, and after that, maybe you'll jump into Cliff's," Nigel added.

"See, we're quite confident that the answers lie with them," Nathan said, "and you present the only way to gather that information."

My fear began to subside, replaced by excitement at the thought that I could communicate with either Ben or Cliff. "Will they know I'm there?" I asked. "Will I be able to talk with them?"

Nigel immediately added some additional rules. "Most likely they'll sense that something is off. But, no, you won't be able to communicate with them. Don't try. It could be devastating for them."

"What am I trying to find out?"

"You'll see things from their perspective. They are both carrying a heavy burden right now. Cliff is responsible for horrific deaths and Ben…"

Nathan slapped Nigel on the arm, and Nigel abruptly stopped speaking.

"Ben what?" I said. And then I said it again: "Ben what?"

"Come on, Nigel! You can't fucking do that!" Nathan was almost yelling.

Nigel persisted: "Ben, he doesn't want to be alive anymore. I'm sorry, Maggie. He just doesn't want to be there. He wants to be here." Nathan was dismayed, but I was relieved to know what was happening.

"What's he going to do?" I asked. Again, I was pleading for information.

"He's a loose cannon," Nathan said. "We don't think it's going to end well for him—and possibly that will affect others as well."

"Could I change that?"

"Yes, you could," Nathan said, firmly. "And if you do that, you'd be helping everyone else. This is your time, Maggie. This is our time. It's time to put an end to Cain and PopCon. It's over for them, and their demise will begin right through this door." Nathan walked over to the door and propped it open.

So, I'd be venturing into the unknown once again.

CHAPTER ELEVEN

I stood up, and walked toward the open door, moving slowly. Nigel followed me. I looked back at him, and he nodded with apparent approval, his eyes shining. *The eyes don't lie,* I told myself.

I stopped at the doorway and took a few deep breaths. This was the entrance to another room, and Nathan was already inside, indicating that I should join him. There was one piece of furniture, a pod-shaped chair that stood alone in the middle. It looked like an adult-sized baby swing. It reminded me of the baby swing that had been passed down from Ben to his brothers and to Reese. It was quite simple—no buttons or lights—and it looked extremely comfortable. This chair was a place for me to get into the zone, or whatever it was that I needed to get into to perform a soul jump. I guessed that I would be engaging in something similar to the practice of meditation.

Nigel now stood beside the pod, and he motioned for me to get into it. "You'll need to reach deep into your mind," he said, "and to become oblivious to your surroundings."

I was still a little worried. "What happens if something goes wrong? Will I be OK?"

"You'll be fine," Nigel said. He knelt beside the pod and took one of my hands as I sat in it. Nathan had remained in the doorway, which was about twelve feet away. I looked at him and smiled. I was quite comfortable.

"I've done this before," Nigel told me in a whisper that Nathan wouldn't be able to hear. "You may see some things you don't want to see."

"What do you mean?" I asked, also whispering. "Will I be hurt?" I squeezed Nigel's hand and lifted my head.

"Stay down and be calm," Nigel said. "I don't want Nathan

coming over here. You won't get hurt, but don't jump into Ben's soul. Just observe from the outside." Nigel's one good eye was burning into me as he gave me clear instructions to do the opposite of what Nathan had told me to do.

"Everything OK, guys?" Nathan called out. He was still standing at the doorway.

"I'm good," I said to put him at ease. "I'm good," I said again—but I wasn't good. I was terrified. But I was still in. "Let's do this," I said.

"Let everything occur naturally," Nigel said, still whispering. "Don't fight whatever happens. If you fight it, that's where things can go wrong."

"How will I know if something is going wrong?" My heart was racing.

"I can't explain it, but you'll know. If you feel it's going wrong, snap yourself out of it. That's all I know. That's what I did, and I came back perfectly fine. I have to go now." Nigel released my hand and patted me on my knee; then he walked back to the door.

"We'll be able to hear and see you behind this door. You'll be fine, Maggie, I promise." Nathan tried to soothe my fears.

When I was six, we took a family trip to the Ohio amusement park, Cedar Point. It was July 4th weekend, and, as expected, the park was packed with families enjoying the beautiful weather and the many roller coasters. Even though I was just six, for some reason I remember every detail of this trip. I believe that's because of the wide spectrum of intense emotions I experienced. At one moment we were extremely happy and the next I feared for my life.

Every bit of the trip was perfect. From the drive up to Ohio to fast-food pit stops and, of course, the park itself. My father refrained from drinking, which, now that I think back on it, was shocking. My mother was grinning from ear to ear the entire trip as the family moments that she desperately hoped for were actually becoming a reality. Martin was only two, but was the perfect little guy the entire time. He took in all the fun sights at the park and even got to ride on a kiddie roller coaster tucked into my father's lap. When that ride stopped, we had a fellow park goer snap a photo of the four of us. I know exactly where that photo is—in the album on a bookshelf next to my bed. That same bookshelf was spattered with blood from the awful night of my murder.

After the photo was taken, I rode some of the smaller coasters with my father while my mother and Martin waited. Then Mom and Dad alternated riding the bigger coasters by themselves while the other watched me and Martin. While my mother was riding the biggest coaster in the park, the Adrenaline Rocket, I asked my father if I could use the restroom. Normally, he'd walk over with me and stand outside, but the restrooms weren't very far away, and he felt I could handle this on my own. I was on my way to the restroom when I saw the park's mascot, Pointer, heading my way. He was tossing little miniature versions of himself out to little kids as he made his way down the park's main drag. Rather than go straight to the restroom, I followed Pointer, trying to catch one of his dolls. It took a while, but I finally caught one of the toys. I clutched the stuffed animal with joy. I couldn't wait to show my parents. However, in my focus on securing a toy, I had followed Pointer through the park for quite a while. I was now lost in an amusement park with thousands of strangers. I looked around, but nothing was familiar.

At first, I was afraid I was going to get in trouble with my parents because I had wandered off. But then I was just afraid. How was I going to find them? I had never been alone like this before. To be alone, truly alone, for the first time in your life is terrifying. Through the eyes of a six-year-old, this park was enormous and full of strange people. Panic set in as I tried to get my bearings. I had no idea what direction I had come from. I must have appeared lost to the families that quickly passed me by, but no one stopped to help me, and I certainly wasn't going to ask a stranger for assistance.

Tears began to roll down my cheeks, but still no one offered their assistance. More than an hour had passed since I made my trek to the restroom, my father now regretting his decision to allow me to go alone. My mother finished up her ride on the Adrenalin Rocket only to find a panicked father and me missing. Of course, they thought the worst had happened to me. They jumped to the horrific conclusion that I had been kidnapped.

Alone at six and again at forty-four. The fear that had run through me so long ago was running through me right now. I don't like being alone anymore. I was taking a leap of faith that this soul jumping was the right thing to do and that it would eventually put an end to my loneliness. That scared little girl wandering around a crowded amusement park was here with me right now. She had made it through a couple of hours of Hell and uncertainty that ended with an ecstatic reunion with her parents. No one was angry with me; my parents were both pleased that I was safe. Now, I was hoping for another reunion—a reunion that also ended in happiness. I was taking a step toward making that happy ending a reality. I closed my eyes and let myself drift into deep meditation. I didn't know where I'd end up, but I was allowing my hope of a happy reunion to push me forward.

Whatever I was doing appeared to be working. I could feel the temperature in the room drop. Before very long there were goose bumps on my arms, and my teeth were chattering. The room began to freeze. I tried to ignore this discomfort, taking Nigel's advice to not fight, to just let things happen. Even after the cold became uncomfortable, I used my mind to rise above my physical reactions in this phase of my soul-jumping journey.

My hands were tightly interlocked in my lap, and my head was pressed back into the pod. I started imagining what I'd learn by jumping into Ben's soul—and how my new knowledge might help him, and also help us in our battle against PopCon. My mind was being drawn down this path, and I could feel the room begin to warm up again. I had lost my intense focus which seemed to change the climate of the room. I took a deep breath and started over. After a few deep breaths, I seemed to be back on the right path—the air temperature again dipped, the goose bumps and chattering teeth came back. I remained in that state for what felt like an eternity. I was now accustomed to the temperature to the point where my clenched hands began to sweat. I removed my hands from one another, stretching my fingers out and placing them on the sides of the pod, or what I thought would be the sides of the pod. To my surprise, my hands fell by my side with no impediments. I tested this freedom with my legs as well and nothing was there. The pod was gone, and I was floating. I took another deep breath and saw that my heart rate continued to drop. The cold room and my deep meditation had slowed my heart rate to a pace that wouldn't have been healthy for a living being. My eyes remained closed, but I could see a bright light through my eyelids. I decided to take a chance and open my eyes.

I felt blinded. The light was so intense. It was the way you feel when a light is switched on in a completely dark room—your eyes need to adjust. In that way, my eyes needed to adjust to this light. In a few minutes, my pupils had shrunk, and I could see what was before me. There was my son Ben, sitting with my sister-in-law, Lisa. They were at Lisa's kitchen table enjoying a Saturday morning breakfast of pancakes, eggs, and bacon. Ben's cousins—the twelve-year-old twins Sophia and Charlie Junior—were also at the table. Charlie Senior had probably left hours earlier for his job at the local country club.

Other than my terrifying vision of Ben that I'd seen on my journey to Gateway, this was the first time I had seen my eldest son since the night of the murders. He was wearing flannel pajama pants with a wife-beater tank top. There was a gnarly scar on his arm from where the claw portion of the hammer had penetrated it. It was miraculous that there was no deep, permanent damage—though he must have been scarred inside, and the scar on his arm would always remind him of the horror he went through that night. Ben saved his own life. He couldn't possibly have saved anyone else because he was the last one Cliff went after. I can't know what was going through Cliff's mind that night, but there were a few obvious reasons why he might have left Ben for last. Ben was big for seventeen. Cliff had to know Ben could have been   a threat to his plan. The other practical reason for Cliff to go after Ben last was the placement of Ben's room, which was the farthest from our bedroom. It was obvious that Cliff would go after me first. Right now, I was thinking of a third reason for Ben's being last: Ben's intense will to live.

I watched the four of them at the breakfast table, chattering back and forth about what their Saturday had in store. Ben loved his twin cousins, and his smile showed it. Ben smiling brought tears to my eyes. What I was seeing in this moment is what I'd been wanting for Ben: for him to be happy. Nathan and Nigel had told me that Ben was not happy. That wasn't what this scene was saying—though I suppose that the good feelings I was seeing in this moment might be fleeting. I just wanted to keep Ben smiling. I wanted him to live a long and happy life, putting this tragedy behind him. Still, I knew how challenging that would be for him. He was about to graduate from high school, although he'd taken a break from school. He had attempted to go back right away, but it was simply too much for him. His teachers and guidance counselor thought it would make sense to take a little time off. Charlie Senior and Lisa, Ben's guardians, agreed. Ben had been assisting Charlie Senior at the golf course to earn a little money but also—and more importantly—to get him out of the house. Ben hated being alone and now he found himself solo too often. The twins would go to school while Charlie and Lisa went to work. Ben had picked up the practice of writing in a journal, which he found cathartic. The question that was weighing on him now was whether or not to visit his father in jail. Charlie Senior had been talking against this idea, while Lisa was of the opinion that a visit could help Ben move forward.

On the night of the murders, Cliff had confessed his guilt. He explained what had brought on the rage that killed most of his family. It was me and my wrongdoings that had pushed him over the edge. With his admission of guilt, there would be no trial. There would just be his sentencing. It was scheduled for about four weeks from now. Ben would surely see his dad at the sentencing as the boy had been asked to speak. The district attorney was pushing for the death penalty and was likely to get it. Of course, many appeals would take place between the sentencing and any potential lethal injection. Tennessee could also repeal the death penalty entirely, which would be motivation for the district attorney to move this case along quickly.

To the prosecutor, this was an open and shut case—Cliff had owned up to the murders. It's rare to ask for the death penalty when someone has confessed, but the gruesomeness of this case—a man killing his own children—gave it a special place in public opinion, which was solidly against Cliff. After the sentencing, the prosecutor would try to move the case through the appeals as quickly as possible. Cliff had no interest in appealing, but his attorney, Max Sunderland, did. Mr. Sunderland had said he'd taken Cliff's case pro-bono, because he wanted to represent a man who was clearly insane at the time of his crime. This wasn't actually why he'd taken the case. As everyone knew, this case came with a tremendous amount of local, national, and even international publicity. It was the kind of case that could catapult Mr. Sunderland's career into the Johnnie Cochran stratosphere—Cochran being the man who had defended O.J. Simpson in his murder trial by saying, "If it doesn't fit, you must acquit." Cliff was no celebrity defendant, but his crime was so horrific that he'd taken on a celebrity status whether he wanted it or not.

"Charlie, Sophie, please give us a minute," Lisa motioned for the kids to head into the family room where they could watch TV.

"What now?" Ben asked. He knew that Lisa liked to take

advantage of the time Charlie Senior was away to advance her case about Ben visiting his father.

"You know what," she said. "I think you should reconsider seeing your father before the sentencing."

"How's he doing?" Ben asked.

"About as well as you'd think a person in his situation could be." I was shocked to realize that Lisa had been to see Cliff.

"Is he remorseful at all?"

"Of course, he is, Ben. As a matter of fact, he's suicidal. I think your visit would help him a lot." Lisa seemed overly concerned about Cliff's well-being, which came as a surprise. She had never seemed to like Cliff, and now she was defending him—as a murderer!

"Why? He'd probably just get upset seeing me alive. He didn't finish the job." Oddly enough, Ben chuckled.

"Take that back, Ben. That's awful. I'm telling you, he's a mess and could use your help. Do you want him to die?" I thought Lisa was laying it on a little thick. Was Ben supposed to feel guilty for his father's state of mind?

"Yes, I want him to die! I wish I could have killed him that night. He's ruined my life, and you want me to help him! Someone should be helping me!" Ben was shaking. He stood, ready to walk away.

"I'm sorry, Ben." Lisa got up, too, and placed herself between Ben and the door to the family room.

"I don't want to see him," Ben said, looking straight into Lisa's eyes. "Please don't make me do it."

"OK, OK. I'm sorry. That's the end of this conversation. It's settled. I'm sorry." Lisa hugged Ben then. She must have known that her passion for this had crossed a line.

Witnessing Ben's pain and not being able to console him hurt my soul. My emotions began to take over now, and I noticed my vision was becoming blurred. My lack of focus was impacting my ability to stay in Ben's world. I composed myself, and my vision was restored. Being able to control my emotions had been a powerful tool for me throughout this journey in the afterlife—and even before. In my life, I had been typically even keeled, providing a voice of reason in our family on many occasions. Cliff, on the other hand, had quite a temper. I'd never imagined that his temper would erupt as the fit of rage he'd unleashed on my family that night.

I saw that this was the first time since my death that I'd referred to the family as *my* family. I'd had trouble taking a firm stance against Cliff, knowing that I was the cause of his outrage. Hearing Lisa's perspective and her clear compassion for Cliff was a surprise, but I also found it comforting. I was beginning to think that I was crazy for thinking that Cliff was anything other than a monster. But now I could see that I was not the only one with a soft spot for a man who was an admitted murderer of his own children. Lisa's insistence that Ben visit Cliff angered me, but I could see that I had to keep those feelings in check if I was going to continue on here. My mission was still a mystery to me. I was simply observing my son with the hope of learning something I could share with Nathan and Nigel. So far, nothing had struck me as being odd. I felt like a potted plant, sitting as I was and watching interactions I have no control over. Ben sat back down and worked on finishing his breakfast. Actually, he was pushing food around on his plate with his fork.

"Mom, I'm sorry for what I did." Ben was speaking aloud, holding his head in his hands, with his elbows planted on the table. "I'm sorry for Reese, Todd, and Christopher too."

I was amazed. I shouted in response: "Ben, do you know I'm here?" He gave no reaction. He didn't hear me. I continued to observe him the way Nigel had told me to.

Ben kept on talking, whispering—apparently to himself. "I wish I knew what to do. What's the right thing to do?"

I could do nothing to console him. I began to tear up. This was hard for Ben, and this was just the beginning. After the sentencing, he'd have to go through endless appeals. Dateline and 48 Hours had already come calling to interview the "Hero Left Behind," as Keith Morrison referred to Ben. Charlie and Lisa had refused the interview requests on Ben's behalf, but that didn't stop stories from being aired on both shows. I was embarrassed that my family was being portrayed in this sensationalized fashion for the TV watching audience and the media blood suckers. Not to mention the personal attacks on me. I'd been called "whore," "homewrecker," "bitch," "slut," and other choice epithets. "Selfish" was the term that I could most readily agree with. I certainly wasn't a whore. Brent was only the second person I had ever slept with, and I suppose that may have contributed a bit to my infidelity. Sometimes I regretted not having been a whore. Well, not that I wished

I'd been a *whore*. But I do regret that I hadn't had more experience before I jumped into marriage and kids. By "experience," I don't mean just having sex with other men. I missed out on so much of what life has to offer by rushing to get married and start a family. In the long run, I believe that's what hurt our marriage the most. Cliff and I drifted apart as husband and wife. We lost the spark that we'd had before the kids came. Our focus was only on them, leaving no time for the two of us to simply enjoy each other. I know we're not the first couple—nor will we be the last—to fall victim to this diminishment of interest. But usually, divorce is the result and not a quadruple homicide.

Now, poor Ben was left to deal with all of it. He spoke at our joint funeral and watched the tears run down everyone else's face in the church—but not one tear escaped from his own eyes. He'd always been a strong kid. Now he's becoming a man faster than he otherwise would have. He's in an adult world whether he wants to be or not. I think Lisa would more than likely homeschool Ben for his final year in high school, and then he'd be able to escape to college. They'd decided to change his last name to shield him from any further attention when he arrives at what would most likely be the University of Tennessee. With all of the media attention, he won't be able to hide completely. Still, it couldn't hurt to change his name. The Pennington blood will continue to live inside him, but the name will die as soon as the court approves the change. Cliff had three boys who could have carried on his family name, but that's over.

Ben took a deep breath and gathered himself. I followed him as he walked to his room—a characterless guest room in Charlie and Lisa's home. I wished that Lisa would do something to make Ben feel more at home in the room. Probably that would change once he was allowed to go back into his old house. Since that night, crime scene tape had been looped around the property and the place had been under twenty-four hour police surveillance.

Ben collapsed onto the bed, facing up with his arms crossed over his chest. To my surprise, a smile began to play on his face. Was he able to sense that I was in the room? I moved to the side of the bed and caressed his hand. I felt nothing, and neither did he, apparently. He popped up again, diving into the nightstand and pulling out what looked like a journal. He picked up a pen and started scribbling quickly in this journal, writing so fast that the words were illegible. I hovered over his shoulder, watching, wondering if what he was writing might be legible to him. It wasn't to me. He turned to start writing on the third page, and the frantic scribbling slowed down. He began printing block letters: M, followed by an A and an R. There was a sound outside the bedroom door, and Ben looked up. The noise stopped, and he continued writing: S then H, then A followed by two L's. Marshall. Ben put down the journal, and almost immediately I was back in my pod at Gateway.

CHAPTER TWELVE

The drop in temperature was the first clear sign that I had arrived back to my pod at Gateway. My eyes opened to a fuzzy view of two people rushing to my side. Nathan and Nigel were anxious to hear all the details of my trip. My body and mind felt as though I had just come out of surgery and the anesthesia was wearing off. The process of reentry was taxing, but the horror of what I had witnessed overwhelmed me, leading to a shrieking that I had never heard come out of my own body.

"They got him, they got Ben. Please God, no!" I was clutching the sides of the pod still unable to see clearly.

"Calm down, calm down Maggie. We're here." Nigel caught hold of my right hand and released it from the side of the pod.

"Why is this happening? He's all I have left. No, please no!" I continued to scream uncontrollably as my legs began to regain feeling.

"We can help, Maggie," Nathan told me, standing on my other side. "All is not lost, I promise."

For the first time since arriving in the afterworld, I began to feel sorry for myself. Up until now, I had ignored most of my emotional pain, understanding that it would only serve as a distraction. I had been like a horse with blinders—focused only on where I was headed. For me that was the finish line. One by one things came up that would usually crush me emotionally. I brushed them off and focused on the task at hand: how was I going to reunite with my children in Heaven. Ben was my last true connection to the life I left behind. Seeing him violated—in the way he seemed to have been—deflated my once fierce passion. I felt beaten down; I was ready to surrender. If PopCon had set out to destroy me, they succeeded. Proceeding in this crazy afterworld was no longer an option for me. I was already dead, but all I wanted to do was to die again. The pain was more than I could bear, and I no longer had the confidence that this journey would be ending anytime soon.

"Well, then help me!" I yelled at Nathan and Nigel, moving my arms so that they couldn't touch me.

"Calm down, Maggie." Nigel stepped back.

"I'm fucking done with this. All I feel is pain, and neither one of you has helped me yet. I'm not going to be your pawn anymore. I'm leaving!" I pushed myself up from the pod. As my legs hit the floor, I could see that I still felt a little wobbly.

Nathan positioned himself in front of me, attempting to block my path. "How can you leave now?" he said. "We're so close."

"Close? Close to what? If you want to help me then extinguish my soul. I don't want to feel this pain anymore. I've had enough. Can you help me with that? Kill my soul. Get rid of me forever. Send me to Hell for all I care. I want this to end!"

"Are you really going to give up?" Nathan looked at me like a disappointed parent.

"Yes!" I closed my fist and swung as hard as I could, punching his left cheek as hard as I could. To my surprise, that sent him to the floor. He wasn't knocked out, but I'd gotten my point across.

Nigel dropped to his knees next to Nathan, and I walked past them. "Stop, Maggie," Nigel said. "Don't you want to save Ben?"

"Of course, I do! But you assholes have done nothing to help me do that." I stormed through the door headed to the exit. "I'm going to find Marshall out there and put an end to this."

"Get her!" Nathan yelled at Nigel.

Nigel ran behind me, yelling, "Maggie!"

I looked over my shoulder and saw he was gaining on me. "Just let me go!"

"Listen to me, Maggie. Just listen!" Nigel and I reached the exit at the same time. He knew, of course, that I wouldn't be able to open the door by myself. I was trapped here until Nathan or Nigel allowed me to leave.

"No, you listen to me. Open this fucking door. I'm done with being your savior." I was eye-to-eye with Nigel as we happened to be about the same height.

"What's out there for you, Maggie? Tell me that." Nigel lowered his voice and spoke to me as if I were a friend, a reasonable person— and not the screaming harridan I'd been acting like.

The change of tone worked. I sat down on the floor with my back against a wall and pulled my knees into my chest. My head dropped down then, and the tears began to flow. Even trying to get out of this place was impossible. Nathan and Nigel had shown me kindness, which had seemed to be genuine, but I didn't care. I wanted to remove myself from this situation. The fact was that I had no idea where I'd go if I got out of Gateway. I was like a kid. It wasn't that I wanted to go someplace; I just wanted to run away from here—from *this*!

I heard footsteps going in the other direction which prompted me to lift my head. I wiped my tears away with the back of my hand— the same hand I had used to punch Nathan. Nigel was walking away from me. He knew I couldn't leave and perhaps he thought it best to give me some time to think. I shut my eyes once again and dropped my head between my knees. I took a few deep breaths, inhaling through my nose and out my mouth. I began to get my wits about me once again.

"God, what do I do now?" I spoke aloud, hoping to receive a sign of some sort.

I heard a pair of footsteps approaching. Nigel and Nathan were walking toward me.

Nathan was the one to speak. "We discussed this, and it's not right for us to keep you here against your will. That's not what we are about."

Behind me, the door opened. The sunlight filled the room, and a light breeze began to flow through, slightly moving my hair. Although it had actually been just a short time, I felt like I had been behind the doors of Gateway for days and days. I got up, looked outside, and then turned again to face the two men I'd been seeing as my captors.

"Thank you, both," I said, taking a deep breath. "Really, thank you. I think I have to do this on my own."

"What are you going to do?" Nigel asked.

"I'm going to find Marshall. I'm going to stop him from destroying the only child of mine still living. And I'm not going to stop until Marshall and anyone else out there who is trying to harm Ben leaves him alone to live his life." I turned around and walked out the door.

As I left, I heard Nathan say in an undertone, "Let Monty know she's coming and send someone behind her." Then the door closed.

Once again, I found myself alone. My only option was to backtrack toward the Vulture Circles. I was confident that a sign would present itself along the way. That was what had usually happened before. However, every time I'd thought that I'd gotten a handle on this place, something new would come up, something that rained on my parade. I realized that I had felt comfortable at Gateway—anyway, as comfortable as I'd felt anyplace in the afterworld. But I also felt like I was wasting my time there. Their mission was good—but it was a mission for the future, not for the present. Nathan and Nigel meant well, but their goal wasn't to save Ben. They would be OK with saving Ben, if it worked out that way. But that wasn't what was moving them—and it was what was moving me. It was my purpose.

On the other hand, I wasn't completely truthful with Nathan and Nigel. Yes, my reason for leaving them was mainly because I wanted to find Marshall and protect Ben. But I could see that my curiosity had also contributed to my departure. Someone or something had placed me here and I needed to find out why. It would be easy for me to make a beeline back through the Memory Pool and the Path of Lost Souls for another shot at making it into Heaven, but that was not why I was here. Once I could figure out why I was here, I'd be able to rest in peace—hopefully, with my family in Heaven.

Until then, I was hyper-focused on defining my purpose, and the first step was to find Marshall.

CHAPTER THIRTEEN

Whoever was creating this world had a sick mind. I hadn't been at Gateway for an extended period of time, but everything outside of Gateway now looked different from when I'd first arrived. My ability to navigate had always been strong, but without sufficient landmarks even the best navigators can get lost. The sun continued to be my guide, and I'd been using Monty's clock dial as my way to navigate from place to place. I'd checked off three of the four locations on the clock dial with PopCon being the only one remaining.

The sun was almost directly overhead as I began my trek south. I figured that I'd need to confront the PopCon leadership to get the answers and results I'm searching for. I'd been on the steps of Hell, ventured into the unknown at Gateway, been denied at Heaven's gate— so, all that was left was PopCon. Surprisingly enough, I feared PopCon more than any of the other three destinations. Everything I'd learned about PopCon told me that evil dwelled there.

The once-wooded terrain that I was navigating became a swampy mess. My footwear had been gone the moment I left Gateway, along with my older appearance. I was a barefoot teenage girl once again. I'd grown to like the look. For some reason it made me feel invincible. I suppose I felt that way because that's how I had felt as a teenager. For better or worse, teens tend to feel invincible. That's why all of us perform some of our dumbest and riskiest stunts as teenagers. That's also why our parents were often scared to death when we, as teens, were out with friends, driving around in cars, or experimenting with a few drinks. Our parents knew how vulnerable we were, but the teenage mind does not know vulnerability—and this can lead to devastation. Cliff knew about this all too well. As long as I'd known Cliff, he remembered like it was yesterday the death of his brother, Russ, and Russ's girlfriend, Sarah.

It happened just three weeks before Russ and Sarah were to walk across the stage at Western Hills High School as proud graduates. They had been dating for just a year. Their time together was coming to an end because Russ was going to be heading to Austin to start school at the University of Texas, while Sarah was going to the University of Florida on a volleyball scholarship. The two had met because of athletics. Russ had been an outstanding baseball player, and he turned down scholarships from several out-of-state schools for the chance to join the storied UT program. Sarah had multiple offers as well, including a partial scholarship to UT. Florida came up with a better offer, though, and she took it. She knew that this decision was likely to be the end of her first love. It was a tough decision for Sarah, but her parents nudged her to go to Florida—not because they didn't like Russ, but because they felt it was the best move for Sarah.

Baseball season had just ended for Russ with an unfortunate surprise ousting in the playoffs. As a four-year starter and team captain, it was a sad time for Russ. He was turning a page not knowing whether he'd play another inning. As was customary at the end of each season, the players were planning to gather for an end-of-year party without parental guidance. The party location was never revealed until the day itself to avoid unwanted guests and, more importantly, parental spying or interference.

The previous three parties had been broken up by the police before getting out of hand. The police were tipped off by the parents. This was the game that was played between the kids and the parents. The kids planned the party while the parents tried to figure out where it was going to be so that they could thwart it as early as possible. Some of the guys weren't even allowed out of their houses on the night of the party. Maybe these parents were being a bit overprotective, but that's how they chose to handle it. They were wary—and there was history. The team had once been suspended for the first four games of the following season due to vandalism, underage drinking, and an overall disregard for the neighborhood in which the party was held. The parents continually reminded the players of that night with the hope of scaring them straight. Why would they want to forfeit any games the following season!

This year, to throw parents off the scent, the kids had gotten creative with the party's location. Russ and a few of the other players had become friends with a player from a local private school. Ryan was the

111

star of Fort Worth Country Day. Russ and Ryan had played together on the fall travel team for the past three years. They were teammates in the fall and rivals in the spring, but friends in the end. Ryan was awaiting Major League Baseball's June draft in which he'd certainly be a first-round pick. This six-foot-five, left-handed pitcher could consistently throw the ball at just under a hundred miles an hour, making him a hot commodity for the major league scouts.

Luck would have it that Ryan's parents were out of town the weekend of the Western Hills baseball year-end party. Russ learned that Ryan would have his house to himself that weekend. Russ floated the idea, and Ryan jumped at the chance to host the party. Ryan's girlfriend went to Western Hills, so Ryan felt like he was part of the gang already, and he thought that hosting this party would be a lot of fun. His parents' home was on ten acres of land, and the nearest neighbors wouldn't even know there was a party going on.

In every other way, this was a typical high school party—loud music and lots of beer. The real entertainment came from watching everyone play quarters and other beer-drinking games. Most of the guys had girlfriends and, for the ones who didn't, there were plenty of single girls who tagged along to be a part of what was sure to be an epic party. After all, there was a keg. Having a keg meant that the party host meant business.

The party was exactly what the guys had hoped for. No parents, no fights, and plenty of beer. Russ and Sarah planned to spend the night at Ryan's house as did most of the other players on the team. None of them had their parents' permission to stay out, but they figured they'd ask for forgiveness rather than permission.

It was just past midnight when one of the guys suggested that they go on a run to Taco Bell. This was a favorite place with the kids. To determine who would make the run, the guys played a game of quarters with the loser deemed the Taco Bell runner. By this time, all of the guys were at least ten beers deep. Their girlfriends pleaded with them to have some pizzas delivered instead, but the guys responded by chanting, "Taco Bell...Taco Bell." In the game of quarters, Russ drew the short straw. As he made his way to the driveway, Sarah caught hold of his arm and pleaded with him not to get in the car. "I'm fine," Russ told her. "Don't worry." She tried to insist on driving—she'd had less to drink than he had—but Russ got into the driver's seat, intending to head out alone. Sarah planted herself in the passenger front seat, telling Russ that she didn't want him to go, but if he insisted, then she was going with him.

Ryan's house was on a secluded road with no streetlights. Russ drove with his lights on high so he could see better. He knew he was drunk and needed all the help he could get. He'd gone about a mile and a half—half the way to the nearest Taco Bell—when a vehicle approached from the opposite direction. Russ forgot that he had his high beams on. As the other vehicle moved closer, it veered over into Russ's lane and accelerated. Whoever this was wanted to play chicken—the loser swerves first. Sarah screamed at Russ to pull to the side. Instead, Russ accelerated as well. He was playing along. Sarah started hitting Russ on his right arm, screaming for him to stop. The cars sped down the road at each other, neither ready to blink. The driver of the approaching vehicle also had put his high beams on as well. Blinded, Russ wasn't giving in, and Sarah could see that this would end in disaster. She took hold of the wheel and yanked it toward her hard. It worked, the car swerved, and Russ slammed on the brakes. They came to an unceremonious halt on a grassy shoulder. Sarah was stunned and a little banged up, but relieved. Their lives had been spared.

But Russ hadn't had enough. He wheeled the car around in a hard U-turn, slammed the gas pedal to the floor, and took off after the other vehicle, a pick-up truck. Sarah was screaming at him, pleading for him to stop. Russ ignored her. His Volkswagen Golf was moving down the country road at just over ninety-five miles an hour; the steering wheel was shaking from the momentum. When they were about twenty yards away from the truck, the other driver put on his brakes. Russ did the same, but it was too late. He and Sarah slammed violently into the back of the truck. The front of the Golf collapsed, crushing both driver and passenger. They died instantly. Just like that, two promising young adults were dead.

The two teenagers in the pick-up truck, the ones who had started the dangerous game of chicken, were unharmed. They walked away with a few bumps and bruises and, of course, the guilt of having been at least partly to blame for two deaths. The two in the truck were never charged with a crime or officially deemed responsible for the deaths. Because of the speed Russ was traveling, he was seen as the cause of the crash. Also taken into account was Russ's blood alcohol level, which was well over the legal limit. The other two boys had been drinking, but they weren't legally drunk. They were teenagers who had made some bad decisions on the road. Ironically, they were headed over to Ryan's house with an order from Taco Bell that they had just picked up.

This accident was a nightmare for Russ's parents—who were, of course, Cliff's parents as well. A few weeks after Russ's closed casket funeral, his parents put their house on the market and moved Cliff and his younger brother to Franklin. So, it was tragedy that brought Cliff into my life—and another tragedy that tore us apart.

For some reason, Cliff would often tell the story of his brother's death. Cliff had shared this story with our kids several times with the hope that it would scare them straight. He'd even shared it at the local high school with Ben watching from the audience. I guess it helped Cliff cope with losing Russ, and if telling the story helped save one life, then it was worth it.

CHAPTER FOURTEEN

I continued to trudge through the mess, heading south to PopCon. In the distance I finally saw a familiar area. Vulture Point was approaching, and there I hoped to reconnect with Monty. A few more yards and the terrain gave way to the wheatgrass that helped define Vulture Point. I knelt, waving my hand back and forth through the tall grass, which folded down and rose back up as my hand passed through it. In a world where little was comforting, I latched onto anything I could. This grass helped comfort me. It's how all of this had started: me laying on my back staring at the vultures that were circling perfectly above. I remembered that a strange calmness overcame me just then. I couldn't explain why I'd felt so comfortable when I arrived, but I did. This grass reminded me of that time. I dropped my other knee to the ground and rolled onto my back, staring up into the sky. With everything I'd experienced here since, I needed a moment to let it all go. The light breeze moved the grass around me ever so slightly, back and forth. I found this hypnotic. It was the closest thing to sleep that I'd experienced since I came here. I closed my eyes for a bit. The only sound was the light rustling of the grass.

I opened my eyes, looking directly above me at two vultures circling. Panic set in then, and my heart began to race. The rustling became louder, but the grass wasn't moving any differently.

"Get up!" Monty was beside me, tugging on my arm. "Get up!"

"Are those birds for me?" I asked as we fled from the area.

"No, someone is arriving. We have to get out of here, now!" Monty started running toward the south.

"Who is it?" I asked, trying to keep pace with Monty.

Monty jumped down into a small clearing about three feet below the grassy field. I followed, and then we were hidden from whomever was arriving. The two vultures continued to circle above. Monty had seen this occurrence a number of times, but this was a first for me witnessing an arrival as a bystander. I watched, intent and nervous, while Monty knelt beside me, completely calm. I wanted to find out who was arriving; Monty was planning his first steps with the newcomer. His role here was a combination of a welcoming committee, a guidance counselor, and a tour guide. He took this seriously; he felt that the arriving soul had been sent to him for a reason. Coming to an understanding of this reason, or reasons, was the hardest part of Monty's job. For as long as I'd been here, he still didn't know exactly why I was here or what he needed to do to help me. Generally, he would follow his instincts, and that would lead him to the right course.

"Look!" Monty was whispering. He discreetly pointed to a spot in the field.

"Where?" I tried to follow Monty's finger, but I couldn't pick up on anything in the field.

"You'll see. Just be quiet." He continued to point.

"Oh my God. Who is that? Oh my God," I had known someone was going to arrive, but until I actually saw them peek above the wheat grass, it didn't hit me.

"*Shhh.* Give her a moment." Monty pushed down slightly on my shoulder. I needed to pull back, or I was going to blow our cover.

Up from the grass stood an absolutely stunning woman. Her long auburn hair flowed down to the middle of her back, the light breeze moving through it gently. Naturally, she looked lost. She surveyed her surroundings, turning in a full circle and looking, unknowingly, in the direction of Gateway, Hell, PopCon, and Heaven. The wheatgrass rose up thigh high on her naked body. Her hazel eyes stared into the distance, as if she were searching for answers. This flawless creature almost appeared to be a mirage. She took a deep breath and raised her arms into the air, her beautiful hair covering her naked breasts. Continuing to hold her arms in the air, she leaned her head back as if she were beckoning someone to come down from above to help her. Her mouth was moving, but we were too far away to hear what she was saying. Her arms lowered into prayer while her head remained skyward. I think she was praying, much as I had been when I arrived, she was praying. The vultures had disappeared, and a sense of loneliness and fear began to set in.

"Let her be for a few more minutes before we approach," Monty said, turning to look at me directly.

"Why is she naked? I wasn't when I arrived."

"Actually, you were. You just don't remember. Everyone is, just like birth."

"I'd rather be naked than wear this ugly dress anymore." I was trying to make light of it, but I could feel that what was happening here was significant.

"Just shut up and watch," Monty said shortly. "You might learn something." So much for jokes.

The woman began walking toward the north, one halting step and then another. She was still barefoot but no longer naked. She wore light blue scrubs.

"Stay here. I'll let you know when it's time to show yourself. I don't want to scare her off." Monty caught hold of a root on the side of the hill and pulled himself up so that this new arrival could see him.

I wanted to join him, but this time I listened to what was being asked of me, and I stayed put. Monty slowly made his way forward. The woman was still staring toward the north, but her prayers had ceased. Monty looked like a predator, getting ready to pounce on his prey—and that's what he was. He knew exactly what he was doing. If this woman saw him approaching rapidly, her flight instinct would kick in and she would run. Monty would eventually be able to catch up to her because she would have no idea where she was going. But this would be much easier for everyone concerned if he got as close as possible before he revealed himself. This was his system, and it hadn't failed him yet.

Monty moved so quietly that he made it to within twenty yards of this woman before she saw him. Then, her head jerked to the right. Naturally, she was startled to see another human being here.

"I'm here to help you," Monty told her, raising both of his hands into the air, palms toward her, fingers outstretched. It was a universal gesture; it said, "I am unarmed; I come in peace." Monty said, "Please don't be scared." He had used a similar approach the first time he met me, and, amazingly, it worked. I watched to see how this woman would react.

"Stop," she yelled. "Stay right there!"

"OK, OK, you've got it." Monty stopped in his tracks, happy that she didn't flee.

"I remember you." She turned toward Monty, extending her right arm out pointing with her index finger.

"How do you know me? That's impossible."

"You're Monty. Yes, you're Monty! My mom told me about you. I can't believe this. Oh my God."

I couldn't see her well, but the woman looked like she was about to weep. And Monty—Monty looked like he'd just seen a ghost. They were talking at a lower pitch now, and I leaned my head out. They were looking at each other; they weren't going to see me. And I knew I needed to hear this.

Monty asked the woman, "How do you know me?"

"My mom came here once. Roseanne—don't you remember her?"

I could tell just by looking at him that Monty did remember Roseanne—and from the bleak expression on his face, I don't think she was one of his big successes.

"Yes, I'll never forget Roseanne," Monty said. "Roseanne arrived here knowing a lot about this place. It seemed like she'd been here before—maybe even more than once."

Hearing Monty say this, I got goosebumps on my arms—and I wondered briefly if maybe Monty felt the same way.

"My mom told me she met you when she died. I didn't truly believe her until this very moment. There is a Monty. You do exist." The woman smiled as she said this, and Monty seemed to relax.

"What's your name?" he asked her.

"I'm Elizabeth. Elizabeth Carlisle, but Carlisle is my married name. My maiden name is Hunt." I could see that Elizabeth was actually wearing a wedding band—something I'd never seen in the afterlife. People would wear clothes reminiscent of some time in their life, but jewelry was quite rare.

"Roseanne Hunt. I never got her last name. Boy, was she a stubborn one. Reminds me of someone else I know." I smiled at this. Monty was taking a jab at me.

"Believe it or not, she actually told me to apologize to you if we ever met." Elizabeth took a few steps closer to Monty.

"Really? Why?"

"I suppose because she was stubborn, just like you said. You have to remember that I listened to her intently on this subject but blew it off because I thought she was nuts." Elizabeth laughed, but it sounded wry rather than really amused. Her mom hadn't been making it up.

"I guess she's getting the last laugh, right?" Monty said, smiling.

"Who knows. And maybe she'll come back here one day." Elizabeth looked up to the sky, where the vultures had been flying a few minutes earlier.

"What else do you know about this place?" Monty asked.

"Well, I know I'm dead, and I suppose I'm here for a reason, right?"

"Correct on both counts, but the second item is a bit more challenging. You see, I'm in the dark just as much as you are. Everyone who comes through here is here for a reason. Some I figure out, but most I just shepherd on to the Memory Pool, letting things happen from there."

"Wait, you don't know do you?" Elizabeth looked puzzled.

"Don't know what?"

"Roseanne's alive. She is still alive. That's how I know what I know."

Monty was obviously stunned by this. "What do you mean by 'alive?'" he asked.

"Alive, as in still on Earth. A living human. That's how I know who you are. My mother came back to life." At this point, Elizabeth started explaining her mother's story for Monty.

It seems that as Roseanne grew older, she'd become prone to seizures, which would sometimes stop her heart. On one occasion she flatlined for over three minutes before the doctors were able to bring her back to life. During that three-minute interval, she arrived at Vulture Point and met Monty. Of course, the three minutes on Earth aren't equivalent to the time Monty spent with her. Monty was with her for what would have felt like several hours to the living. That's when Roseanne hastily jumped into the Memory Pool without Monty. What he didn't know was that she had been revived and has been alive ever since. She'd shared her experience with no one other than Elizabeth as she felt others might think she's crazy. A wise decision since her own daughter had thought she was crazy until right now.

"What happened to her after she jumped?" Monty asked. "Did she share that with you?" Monty had jumped into the Memory Pool with many souls, and I'll bet that Roseanne was the only one he hadn't hit the water with hand in hand.

"She said she floated underneath the water, but had no fear of drowning," Elizabeth said. "It was a calming experience for her, but it didn't last long." I was amazed: Elizabeth was describing the first moments of entry into the Memory Pool exactly as it happens.

"Then she revived on Earth?"

"Yes, the doctors revived her. She's been a changed woman ever since that moment, and she hasn't had a seizure since. She thought you might have had something to do with her seizures going away," Elizabeth added with a smile, "but more importantly, she credits you with saving her life."

"Me? How could I save her life?" Monty said, "I thought I'd failed her. It seemed like my biggest failure ever!"

"She said that you shared your story with her," Elizabeth told him, "All about your parents dying. Your story was sad, but it motivated her to stay alive."

"Are you telling me that Roseanne jumped into the Memory Pool with the intention of reviving herself?" This was all new to Monty.

"That's what she told me. She didn't want to die. That's why she jumped without you."

"How did she know jumping without me would work?" Monty said. Clearly the poor man was deeply perplexed. What did all of this mean about the process he had been going through with the souls that came through Vulture Point?

"My mom told me that you were her shepherd. Your job was to guide her through to Heaven, but she didn't want to go. So, rather than tell you that, she decided to take matters into her own hands. That's why she leaped. I guess this hasn't happened before."

I knew that Elizabeth wanted Monty to feel good about what she'd been telling him about Roseanne's journey, but he looked like she had just delivered a body blow.

"This is terrible," Monty said. "What I've been doing is terrible. Perhaps other souls would have had another chance at life if I hadn't interfered—if I hadn't jumped with them. Nobody ever told me to do this. I was just acting on instinct. Well... of course, now I have some more information to go on."

"Monty, my mom also told me one more thing." Elizabeth positioned herself in front of Monty, and he picked up his head and looked directly into her beautiful eyes.

"What else did she share with you?"

"She said that you've suffered enough in life and in the afterlife. Soon you'll need to let go and take your own plunge into the Memory Pool. It's time for you to move on." She paused for a moment, and then she went on. "Stop torturing yourself here. Your family has been waiting for you for a long time. Stop thinking their death was your fault. Because it wasn't." Elizabeth had tears running down her face now. The heart-wrenching story her mother had told her transformed inside her from a tall tale to reality—to something that had actually happened to a person she knew.

I had been moving closer throughout this exchange, and I now stood close enough that Elizabeth saw me. She was shocked to see another being, and I could now tell that both she and Monty had tears in their eyes.

Still, I had to say what I had to say: "We're not done yet, Monty. You promised to help me, we're not done."

Of course, to Elizabeth, my statement came across as extremely selfish. "Who are you?" she said. "And how can you tell a man that he can't be with his family?"

Maybe I was being selfish, but to me it seemed like a necessity of the heart. I fired right back at her: "Monty and I have a deal that doesn't concern you. You can be on your way now. You know where to go, and you can do it alone."

"Hold on," Monty said, his tears gone. "Hold on a minute, both of you!"

"Monty, we have to find Marshall and get to PopCon. We're so close to figuring this out," I pleaded with him. "Please don't quit now."

"*Why*, Maggie?" he asked. "Why should I continue to help everyone? I think it's time to help myself. Elizabeth was sent here for some reason, and perhaps this is it. She came to deliver this important message and free me of this burdensome role I've been shackled with for a very long time. A role, by the way, that I just found out I've been doing wrong." Monty was clearly on Elizabeth's side.

"You're going to move on, knowing what PopCon is all about? I can't believe you'd do that. Listen, I want to move on and find my children more than anyone, but we're not done here." I was speaking directly to Monty as if Elizabeth wasn't even there.

"Why would you do this to him?" Elizabeth said, letting me know that she was, in fact, very much a part of this conversation. "Hasn't he helped you enough?"

"You don't know me," I said directly to her. "You don't know my past." My voice started rising. "Please just stay out of this. You're trying to steer Monty in a direction you think is right, but you don't have all of the details. Do you even care about your mother? If you really do, you'll stop pushing this idea onto Monty."

"Stop it. Who do you think you are? Both of you! I can make decisions for myself and that's what I'm going to do. I don't want to hear another word from either one of you." Monty started walking toward the north, indicating that this conversation was over. At least for now.

Elizabeth and I clearly started off on the wrong foot, and I knew nothing positive would come out of our being adversarial. The tremendous amount of stress and fear this place throws on an individual is too much to bear. She had just arrived, and I had lost track of how long I'd been here—though I knew that it'd been far too long. While Monty headed off to mull over his options, I decided to start over with Elizabeth.

"Look, I'm sorry we got off on the wrong foot. I'm emotionally ragged, and I feel that I'm very close to getting to some kind of closure here. I was concerned about the direction you were suggesting for Monty." I paused for a moment. It really was selfish. "I wanted his help," I finished, knowing just how lame it sounded.

Elizabeth smiled. "I understand," she said. "I've just arrived, and already I'm stressed out. I'm just holding onto the only thing I know about this place. I was supposed to try to make it right for Monty. My mom asked me to do that, and I'm carrying out her wishes as best as I know how." Elizabeth's reasons were compelling, but—selfishly speaking—would be of no help to me.

"Do you care to learn more about this place? I ask that because you may be safer and better off only knowing a little. I've gotten myself in deep and there's no turning back for me now," I was ready to share my knowledge with Elizabeth, but only if I had her permission.

"The way I see it I have three options. One, take a plunge into the Memory Pool on my own, hoping that I'll be sent back to life. Two, jump in hand-in-hand with Monty, not knowing where the journey will take me. Three, listen to what you have to say and join you in your crusade." Elizabeth laid out her options with no particular emphasis.

"And what are you thinking?" I asked, hoping that she'd at least allow me to tell my story.

"Well, none of the options are that appealing, but my gut is telling me to listen to your story. I may get in too deep, but my instinct is strong, so go for it." Elizabeth leaned over and took my hand, giving it a gentle squeeze.

So, while Monty continued to ponder his options just to the north of us, Elizabeth sat intently listening to my story. She'd interrupt with questions, most of which I didn't have the answer to, adding even more credence to my notion of moving forward to solve this mystery. Let's face it, I was recruiting her. Having her on my side could only help my cause. In my mission to find Marshall and confront PopCon, the more trusted souls I had marching forward with me, the better.

I told Elizabeth almost everything. I neglected to share with her my interaction with Phonso. The guilt and embarrassment of that confrontation was too much to bear. Plus, I didn't want her to have a reason not to trust me. Sure, this was a bit deceptive, but I did share everything else with her. Maybe there will be a time to share the Phonso story, but for now I am keeping that one to myself. I still hoped I could somehow make amends to Phonso, but on that, only time would tell. Right now, my existence relied upon my skills of persuasion with two individuals, both of whom were a bit skeptical.

Elizabeth was able to relate to the life drama that had led to my murder. She, too, had gone astray in her marriage, having had an affair of her own. Her situation was not as complicated as mine—she didn't have children at the time, and her affair had lasted only a couple of months. Elizabeth's side relationship was a way for her to get some retribution when she found that her husband was cheating on her with her best friend. An immature response, but one that helped Elizabeth to feel vindicated. Divorce followed along with the end of her friendship. The ex-husband and so-called friend ended up marrying, an outcome that was crushing for Elizabeth for multiple reasons. First, two people she'd trusted had betrayed her, and—even more important—her hopes of starting a family had to be put on hold for the foreseeable future.

The big problem was timing. At Elizabeth's age, she knew that she didn't have time to find a new guy, form a relationship, marry, and then start a family. And since all of that was out of the question, she decided to go at it alone. An IVF with donated sperm was Elizabeth's way to ensure that she wouldn't go the rest of her life without being a mom. She finally became a mother 178 days after her forty-first birthday. Unfortunately, she never got the chance to hold her baby. Elizabeth died during delivery. A blood clot in her leg led to the stopping of her heart. Little Rosie, named after her grandma, emerged from Elizabeth's womb healthy and strong, although Elizabeth had been dead for several minutes. The doctors brought a new life into the world while another one drifted off.

Nothing is easy here. Listening to Elizabeth's story, I saw that we had all suffered through a great deal of pain. Monty's story had been heart-breaking and, now, so was Elizabeth's. I suppose that's why Roseanne took it upon herself to leap into the unknown. Little Rosie needed someone in her life and Grandma Roseanne could provide that guiding light. Why Elizabeth hasn't already sprinted to the Memory Pool without either Monty or me seems odd. If I had been her, I would have jumped right in there, knowing that it had worked for her mom. Elizabeth didn't have much to lose. I was tempted to do it myself—but I've come too far, and there's no guarantee that by making that jump, I'd end up waking up alive on Earth. Other than Ben, why would I do that anyway? I'm needed here, and my other kids were here. Ben and I would reunite one day the right way, not through some magic leap.

Elizabeth and I were wrapping up our conversation when Monty approached, looking confident.

He raised a clenched fist in the air, and said, "I'm with you Maggie. Let's take a run at this." Then he added, "And once it's over, I'm out!"

"Thank you, Monty!" I was elated.

Monty asked, "What about you, Elizabeth? What's it going to be?"

"Maggie shared her story with me," Elizabeth told him. Then she turned to me and said, "Thank you for doing that. Opening up to someone you've just met isn't easy. It's a gripping drama that you're living through, and I want to help.

"But I have my own needs here. My newborn daughter is alive, and I dearly want to be with her. I think she needs me—and so I'm going to take the chance my mom did. I'm going to see if I can go back."

I don't think Monty was pleased with Elizabeth's decision. What he said was, "There's no guarantee that jumping into that pool on your own is going to transport you back to life."

"Of course, there's no guarantee. But there's one thing I know for sure. If I don't try, I'll be left with the unknown. I'll be left with the 'what if.' I can't do that to my daughter. I owe it to Rose to at least try. I'd rather try and fail than to never try at all."

Elizabeth's words had the same confidence that Monty's had. She knew this was the right decision, and I couldn't argue.

"That's fair," I said. "I'd do the same if I were you."

"Well, everyone has made up their minds," Monty said. "That's enough of this sitting around. Time to get busy." Monty was on point. It was time to stop talking and start doing.

I said, "Let's go to the Memory Pool, Elizabeth." I began to walk toward the west with Monty and Elizabeth bringing up the rear.

CHAPTER FIFTEEN

We were about fifty yards into our journey when Monty stopped and said, "This is all I've known for a very long time." He turned toward the east and took what I realized would be his final look at Vulture Point.

Monty was used to being alone, and he had been alone at Vulture Point. Sure, souls like me and Elizabeth would pass through, but that's all we'd do, pass through. After his parents' murder, Monty was alone for most of the rest of his painful life. A few people passed through on his journey, but in the end, when he took his own life, he was alone. He had known nothing but sadness, and I think that's why he was choosing to follow me on my crusade. Elizabeth said it best: trying and failing is better than not trying at all.

All three of us would be wrapping up our time in the afterlife with no regrets, and that's the way it should be. We had all left our lives on Earth with many regrets, and this was our chance to right some of those wrongs. In a way, this was a second chance for the three of us. We each had our own goals, some simpler than others, but goals, nonetheless. We would soon find out if any of us would be successful in reaching our goals—and if any of us would fail. Either way this went for us, we'd learn from it—and we would be better off for the knowledge.

Standing there at the edge of Vulture Point, I could feel that each one of the three of us was deciding that we would not allow ourselves to be held back by the unknown. The unknown can create a tremendous burden, a burden much too heavy for any of us to continue carrying. We would never be free as long as we kept dragging the unknown along with us. "The unknown" is the demon that can appear as your friend and confidant, but that, in reality, only holds you back. We were all finished with being held back. For better or worse, we were leaving Vulture Point behind. It was someone else's turn to shepherd the arriving souls. It was someone else's turn to face PopCon. It might even be someone else's turn to be a mom to little Rosie. Whatever lay before us, that's what we would each be meeting. We started walking again.

The wind was at our backs, and it was more intense than any wind I'd experienced since arriving here. Monty and I glanced at each other, both of us wary. Elizabeth marched on; she didn't know any better. She was thinking only of the possible meeting with her beautiful baby girl. Monty and I were rooting for her now; we felt like we were part of her story. A happy ending would be divine.

As we reached the incline just prior to the edge of the cliff, Elizabeth picked up her pace, going from a brisk walk to a full-out sprint. "This is it, guys," she called. "I'm going!"

Monty and I started sprinting behind her just to wish her well— and to see what would happen after she took the leap.

Elizabeth let out a little cry as she pushed off the cliff and dove into the unknown. Monty and I stood at the edge of the cliff and watched as Elizabeth gracefully plunged into the Memory Pool feet first, her arms raised overhead.

We lost sight of her almost immediately. The pool was rough from the unexplained wind and the water was darker than normal. Neither of us had ever witnessed a plunge from this perspective and didn't know what to expect. Anytime Monty would accompany a soul, he'd hit the water, plunge down about fifteen feet or so, and then find himself right back at Vulture Point. That's all he knew. I had been in the pool twice with two entirely different outcomes. This watching as a bystander was, once again, another outcome.

"What's happening?" My concern grew for Elizabeth as the water started to bubble. It looked as if it were boiling.

"I don't know," Monty said, clearly concerned. "Oh my God."

The outer edges of the pool began to form a counterclockwise current, which circled the entire pool and began to shrink in circumference while rising in height. A small wave became visible at about ten o'clock. The wave started moving faster at nine… eight… seven… All the while this wave was tightening the circumference of the pool. The epicenter of all of this was precisely where Elizabeth had entered the water.

"What do we do?" I asked. "Jump in?" I felt helpless, watching the moving pool below.

"No, this can't be stopped. If we jump in, we risk ruining everything."

The shrinking of the pool continued, the column of water got higher—and somewhere in the middle of all of this Elizabeth's fate was being played out. The column became like a waterspout. It was as high as the cliff but only about fifty yards wide. Monty and I were able to see the floor of the pool, which looked exactly as it should have looked. It was an empty bed with the only oddity being that it was bone dry. It looked like it had been baking in the sun for days and days. The cracks in the base were wide and peeling upward. We backed up several feet from the side of the cliff for fear that the winds would push us forward and over the side to the hard bed below.

Monty spoke again: "I don't know whether to be happy or not at the sight of this."

"Something different is happening," I said. "Maybe that's a good sign for Elizabeth." I was channeling as much positive energy as I could, although I was also afraid that we might upset the balance of this world by going against the grain of whatever was happening here.

The sky had become stormy. The clouds above us opened up, and a downpour ensued while the wind slowed down a bit. I stepped forward to the edge of the cliff to get a closer look. The rain rapidly filled the empty bed below while the spout continued to churn. Higher and higher the water rose against the cliff to the back of this waterspout. Still, there was no sign of Elizabeth.

I turned to Monty. "This is going to push right over the cliff, isn't it?" The rapid rise of the water along with the churning of the spout would be too much for the pool to handle.

"Hold on," Monty said, but I got that he was speaking to the pool, not me.

"Let's get out of here, now!" I called, and I turned east, sprinting away from the pool.

"Go!" Monty yelled, following close behind.

The wind had picked up once again, and we were running right into it. This headwind was so powerful that our strides were barely covering ground. It seemed that outside forces were trying to push us back to the cliff.

"Hold my hand!" I could barely hear Monty's voice, but I found his hand and held on.

We tumbled to the ground as the hurricane force winds pushed us closer and closer to the Memory Pool's cliff. I clutched Monty's hand as hard as I could as we rolled violently over the dirt and grass below us.

"What's happening? Please God, no!" My hand slipped from Monty's, and he was gone.

The wind took Monty right over the edge. And then it came to an abrupt stop. I was only a few feet from being thrown into the pool myself. I crawled over to the edge. Below me, which had originally been over a hundred feet down was now less than ten. The pool had not only risen about ninety feet, but it had also widened by at least three hundred yards. The beautiful green grass and the lovely yellow flowering trees to the west were all underwater. The place looked nothing like it had just an hour earlier.

Once again, my surroundings had changed, and I was alone. I had to wonder whether or not my inclination to go on this adventure had been correct. Or had I contributed to the demise of the only two friends I currently had. The Memory Pool was no longer a pool. It was a massive body of water with only the cliff containing it, keeping it from flooding Vulture Point.

It seemed to me that by allowing Elizabeth to plunge in without Monty accompanying her, we had somehow upset the balance of what had been a fairly serene space. The Memory Pool hadn't looked intimidating, but this body of water certainly did. I looked toward the south and noticed a path I hadn't seen before. This path went as far as my eye could follow; it seemed to be inviting me to take it. I knew what waited for me if I proceeded southward. It was no secret, and it seemed that this must be my destiny. I had checked out west, east, and north; south was all I had left.

My intention had been to face PopCon with Monty, but this world was unpredictable, and I was alone once again. So, this was it. *This* was the sign.

I began to walk along the path, neatly laid out in front of me. PopCon awaited and, hopefully, a meeting with Marshall. This Marshall had a hold on my son, and I wasn't going to let that continue unchallenged. Marshall had to be dealt with accordingly, and this path would lead me to him. Me, the solitary warrior. I reminded myself that it's better to try and fail than to never try at all.

Monty had no choice but to go on. And Elizabeth—I couldn't criticize Elizabeth. She acted according to what she knew: to attempt to get her life back in the same way her mother had and to support a daughter she hadn't yet met. What Elizabeth couldn't take into account was the unpredictability of the afterlife. I don't see how anyone could solve all its riddles. Monty had been a part of this place longer than anyone else that I'd encountered, and he continued to be surprised by the new and strange things happening around him.

Monty had earned a place in my heart. I wished that I could have helped ease his pain. Gazing out into what were now the calm waters of the Memory Pool, I wondered where Monty was and whether or not he was safe. He was as resilient as anyone could be here. I hoped he had one more trick up his sleeve and that I would see him again. Yes, I could have jumped into the water after him, but I doubted it would have helped. I'd been in the Memory Pool twice now, and the only consistency I'd found was inconsistency. He would have done the same thing, I was sure. And I was better off facing PopCon than I would have been if I'd taken another plunge in the Memory Pool. Monty knew that. I was sure of it.

CHAPTER SIXTEEN

The path I was navigating was rocky and only about three feet wide. To my right, the Memory Pool glistened as the sun bounced off of it. To my left, the wheat grass moved ever so slightly. Here I was, taking in another beautiful moment in the afterworld. If I were alive, I'd sit down and give myself a chance to take it all in. But I'm not here for the experience. I'm not here to be a tourist. I'm here to… I stopped short of finishing this thought. Why was I here?

All this time I had been focused on getting to Heaven to be with my kids, but perhaps I'm here for something bigger? I've been prepared to take on a greater responsibility in the hope that whatever I accomplish for others might lead to an ultimate reward for me. That light at the end of the tunnel has kept me going. I knew where this path was leading, and I knew, too, that perhaps I wouldn't return from this trip. That would be OK, though, because then at least I'd know. I'd know I had tried my best. My kids wouldn't be mad at me or disappointed in me if they knew I tried with all of my heart.

This train of thought reminded me of a conversation I'd had with Christopher shortly before the murders. He loved everything about school, and it showed. His passion for solving problems and figuring out how things worked was somewhat unique, and for this reason, his circle of friends was small. Most of the other kids weren't on Christopher's level and this aspect of him scared them off. His socializing consisted mainly of the clubs he was a member of, and the events tied to those clubs. Cliff and I supported everything Christopher did, even if half the time we didn't understand it. Our garage was his workspace. Sometimes he would simply take electronics apart and put them back together again. He wanted to gain an understanding of how they worked, and that's how he learned. One time he got his hands on Cliff's iPhone and disassembled, reassembled, and returned it to Cliff's dresser without his finding out—ever! This was a little secret that Christopher and I shared.

Christopher's circle of friends consisted of nerds. All teenagers, all boys. Of course, it wasn't long before they started noticing girls. Girls noticed them, but for the wrong reasons. Christopher and his friends were the weirdos in the class. I watched this closely because, as a parent, you don't want your children to be left out by the populist kids or to be hurt, either physically or emotionally. I spent time with Christopher discussing this dynamic to assure that he was OK. He never showed signs of not being OK, but I felt it was important to dive into the subject on occasion. Too many times we'll hear about kids being ignored by their parents, friends, or family, only to see them act out later simply to get some attention. Christopher had a good head on his shoulders, but our talks were important, and I felt like I made an impact on him for the better.

Since he was the smart kid in class, others would try to get Christopher to do their homework for them or give them the answers for quizzes and tests. While he was tempted to assist some of the popular kids with the hope of being accepted into their group, he knew better. They were using him. Well, except for Stacy Rodriguez. Stacy's family had moved to Franklin from Miami. While she and her parents had been born in the U.S., her grandparents had made the dangerous trek from Cuba to escape Fidel Castro's repressive rule. Stacy was bilingual with a heavy accent, which was not the norm in Franklin. Her maturity level was well beyond the other girls in the popular clique that she hung around. She saw Christopher as a peer and not as some geeky kid with the answers to the tests. Her so-called friends would ridicule her for the friendly "hello" she'd give Christopher in the hallways at school.

To no one's surprise, Christopher began to develop a crush on Stacy. Who could blame him? She was a smart, caring, beautiful, mature girl. It was clear that her parents raised her right. I'd met her on a few occasions, and I understood Christopher's interest, but I too doubted anything would come of it beyond the cordial hallway greetings. I was shocked when Christopher came to me one day with some very special news: Stacy had asked him out. Yes, she asked him out. Christopher was excited about this but also guarded. My son, the beautiful and kind boy that he is, had his doubts. He told Stacy he had to check on something, and then he came home to his mom to get my opinion. When he shared this news with me, there were so many things for me to be pleased about, but that was the main one—that he wanted my advice. It melted my heart. I had to come back down from cloud nine to absorb what was happening and provide him with sound feedback. I was so proud of him, and what I knew about Stacy gave me the confidence to approve of this upcoming date. I suggested that he go out with her and enjoy every minute of it because he deserved it. Then Christopher went to school the next day and, rather than take my advice, he declined Stacy's invitation. When he arrived home that afternoon, I had assumed the date was set and asked him where they were headed the following evening. I was shocked when Christopher told me he had said no. It was clearly a confidence issue, and I failed to seize the opportunity to build him up. Instead, I told him it was OK and he should only do what felt comfortable to him.

Three days later we were murdered. Like most human beings I have regrets, but this one weighs heavy on me. I should have insisted that Christopher go on that date. I let my soft heart support his decision to not step up to a challenge. I should have used my brain—of course, Christopher could handle going on a date! And if he had, he could have taken that wonderful memory with him. Now, I'm sure he's looking back on it with regrets, regrets a fourteen-year-old should not have to bear.

The decline of the path grew steeper as I moved farther south for my eventual confrontation with PopCon. While alive, I watched a documentary that examined the adrenaline rush that comes in extreme sports. There are athletes who have become addicted to that rush. I was always a wimp when it came to anything extreme. I didn't even like rollercoasters, and the thought of skydiving scared the hell out of me. In the afterlife, however, I was finding myself seeking my next risky move with the excitement of an adrenaline junkie, looking for the next mountain to ski down or the next big wave to conquer with my surfboard. I had lost track of how long I'd been here and, as Monty had made clear, it really didn't matter. All I knew was that I'd changed, and not in some small or insignificant way. I had experienced more excitement in death than I ever had while I was alive. I'd pushed myself to the limit emotionally. Like a heavyweight fighter in a fifteen-round match, I'd take a beating and then come back for more. I'd like to think that the bell for round fifteen was about to ring, and I was ready. In any event, I was quite certain I'd find out how prepared I was shortly.

I felt the rocks on the bottoms of my bare feet, but I walked down the path with no pain. The sun was rapidly disappearing in the west, but I knew that the moon would be my guide. Soon enough the path would break away from the edge of the Memory Pool. I stopped to survey the terrain ahead and noticed then for the first time, a fluorescent green shimmer along portions of the path ahead. I walked another fifty yards and paused again just before what appeared to be rocks shining in the moonlight. The fluorescent green pulsed at a pace similar to a resting heart rate. I bent down to touch one of these glowing rocks. It was warm at first touch and began to get hotter as my hand rested on it. I kept my hand in place for as long as I could, moving it only when the heat was too much to bear.

The rocks ahead were of varying sizes, some as small as golf balls and others the size of grapefruits. I started walking again, keeping my head down and counting the rocks I passed. These rocks were mesmerizing and quite beautiful. It felt like they were a riddle I'd need to solve. I was certain these rocks weren't coincidentally placed along this path. They meant something, and more than likely they meant something important. I reached the ninety-eighth rock and a gap of about ten feet lay ahead. In those ten feet, there were no rocks at all, just smooth terrain. I took a few steps while my counting paused for a brief moment. The fluorescent rocks continued just ahead.

"Maggie!" A voice from the dark cried out. The sound originated from my left and the swishing through the brush picked up considerably. A violent blow across the left side of my face sent me crashing to the ground.

"Stop, please!" I screamed, curling into a fetal position and hoping that I wouldn't be hit again. I was groggy and in no position to defend myself.

"You're done here." A kick to my side took the air out of me.

"Why… why are you doing this?" I continued to hide my face for fear of being hit again.

"Stay away from here, or Ben will pay." The voice was close to my ear as these words were whispered.

Monty, Nathan, and Nigel had taught me a lot in my time here, but I was still learning. One consistent message each had given me was that my mind was the most powerful asset I had and that I should let my mind take charge of my physical being whenever possible. I hadn't actually figured out how to harness this mental power yet—well, not until this very moment. Because I knew who had hit me without seeing my assailant. And once the voice mentioned Ben, I knew I had come into contact with Marshall.

My natural response to being hit unexpectedly was to collapse in fear. I think a lot of people would do the same thing. But that self-protective response is for the living, not for the dead. In that moment, I could see that being dead changed the whole game. Hitting me wouldn't do anything but mess with my mind. I wasn't physically hurt. It was impossible to be physically hurt in the afterworld. Like a schoolyard bully, Marshall used physicality and mental torment to gain the upper hand over his opponents. I gather he'd spent many a moment doing that and has been successful in scaring people. That was about to change.

"You don't get to do this anymore, Marshall." I sprang to my feet as I spoke, and looking at my opponent in the face, I could see that I'd startled him. I didn't know whether that was because I'd talked back to him or because I'd addressed him by his name. But just like that, I had tipped the scale in this mental battle over to my side.

"Stay down, bitch!" Marshall stepped toward me, pushing me in my chest. To his surprise, I didn't budge, and that was when I saw it. His eyes told the whole story. I wasn't afraid, and that was something Marshall wasn't used to.

"No, Marshall, you won't win anymore." I looked right into his brown, terrified eyes.

"You don't understand the consequences, do you?" OK, so once again he was going to use Ben as a threat.

"I understand it all. Now, get out of my way," I stepped to his left, intentionally brushing my shoulder against his. The rocks underneath me began to shine brighter and pulse quicker as I continued down the hill. I didn't look back.

The adrenaline pumping through my body was as intense as an orgasm. My mental state was at an all-time high, giving me the confidence to face the PopCon leadership. While I had won this particular battle with Marshall, I had no assurance that he had relinquished control of Ben. Marshall's lack of retaliation signified a victory for me, but not the ultimate prize that I was after.

The pulsing of the rocks ahead of me slowed down to what I identified as a resting rate. The meaning of these pulsating rocks was another mystery I'd need to solve, but there would be time for that. I had lost count of the rocks with Marshall's interruption. I started again, picking up at ninety-nine. Another eighteen rocks went by and then I looked up. In the distance I could see a silhouette. I stopped in my tracks.

"Who's there? Identify yourself now." I continued to amaze myself. I had gone from a timid, scared little girl to a strong and confident woman. Nothing was going to keep me from my goal.

"Maggie," the man bellowed. He moved a few steps closer.

"Stop right there," I said, raising my hand in the air. "Identify yourself."

"I'm Conrad," he said, continuing to walk toward me, but doing so slowly. "Nathan and Nigel sent me to follow you."

"Why? Why are you following me?"

"To help you. We can't lose you." Conrad was now just a few feet in front of me—a burly man who appeared to be in his early thirties. But of course, I'd learned appearances mean nothing when figuring out someone's age. He had a receding hairline with portions of his red hair intact on the back and sides of his head. His hair was shaved down fairly tight, while his beard was long and bushy. His black T-shirt was about a size too small for his belly, and his worn jeans and work boots had seen their fair share of action. A rare footwear sighting. What I wanted to look at was his eyes, which not only seemed trusting, but looked to be the same age as the rest of him. I let Conrad explain his journey to me.

"We couldn't let you go out here on your own. Nathan told me to watch over you and intervene if it looked like things might get out of control."

"If you were watching over me, then where the hell were you when Marshall attacked me?"

"I'm sorry about that, but I couldn't let Marshall see me. If he saw me, there's a chance that everything we've done up until now would be ruined. He may not look it, but he's a powerful person in PopCon." Hearing that made me feel good. I had scared someone "powerful" by battling him with my mind.

"He has my son," I said. "Did you know that?"

"Yes, and that's why I'm talking to you now. You need to go back to Gateway for another visit to Ben." Conrad reached for my hand, and I put it behind me, where he couldn't get at it.

"Back to Gateway? I've come this far and you're telling me I need to go back?" No way!

"You need to intervene with Ben. We know what Marshall is capable of—especially now that you've scared him. He'll retaliate."

If there was any way for Conrad to persuade me, this was it. I asked him, "What do you mean by 'retaliate?'"

"Come on, Maggie, you know what I mean."

"No, I don't. Tell me. Tell me, now. Stop with the bullshit." I took a step closer to Conrad, locking eyes with him.

"They'll kill him, Maggie. That's what they'll do." Conrad broke eye contact with me and he stared down at the pulsating fluorescent green rocks.

Here I was, dead. While I was dead my actions were still endangering my family. Where is my God when I need him? This place was so cruel that it made me wonder if this wasn't actually Hell. It appeared as if I had no choice. PopCon would have to wait while I reversed course and headed back to Gateway.

I was being challenged once again, only this time my son's life was on the line.

CHAPTER SEVENTEEN

Conrad and I walked side by side. The same rocks were on the path, but they were not a pulsating fluorescent green. I was hoping Conrad might know more about these strange rocks, but he was just as baffled as I was. It was still dark out, and without the glowing rocks our feet did the navigating for us. We'd step off course occasionally, but it was easy to follow the rocky path, which I knew would lead us back to the Memory Pool and then Vulture Point.

Conrad hadn't seen Monty since he fell into the pool, and this saddened me. I prayed that he'd found salvation after the violent winds that followed Elizabeth's leap into the Memory Pool had literally thrown him into the water.

The walk back to the Memory Pool was all uphill and steeper than I'd noticed in my descent earlier. When I'd started walking down this path to PopCon, the pool was a violent mess emitting plenty of noise as the water crashed on the side of the cliff. As we neared the pool now, I noticed that the noise had dissipated. A few more steps and we arrived at the edge of the pool.

When we reached the edge of the pool, I studied it with the help of the moonlight. "It's back to normal."

"Looks to be that way," Conrad said, standing what looked to me to be dangerously close to the edge. I stayed about five feet back.

"Is order restored?" For Monty's sake I was hoping so.

"That's not something we can confirm nor deny. The one thing I've learned while here is that the only consistency is inconsistency." Conrad smiled, perhaps because he had once again declined to answer a direct question with anything of substance.

"Boy, you're pretty useless, aren't you?" I laughed then, and that felt good.

By the time we reached Vulture Point the sun was inching up out of the east. I scanned the area hoping to see Monty, but he was nowhere in sight.

"Let's head over here." I motioned to the spot Monty had me hide at when he approached Elizabeth.

"Maggie, we don't have time for this." Conrad reluctantly followed as I began a light sprint.

I arrived at the edge of the small drop-off and jumped a few feet down. The spot was empty. Monty was gone. That anticipation during that short sprint over only ended in sadness. My heart told me that he'd be there, but my mind knew better. Once again, trust your mind, not your heart.

Still, I felt a responsibility for Monty. He'd done a lot for me. What I said was, "We need to find Monty and take him to Gateway with us."

"Maggie, I'll be as blunt as possible: if you don't get to Gateway soon, Ben will be dead."

"It's that serious, huh?" It was a stupid question.

"Yes, it's that serious." Conrad started walking without me.

I caught up with him, and walking beside him once again, I asked, "Why did they send you?"

"I volunteered," he said, not even looking at me. "This is our chance. It's the best chance I've ever seen." Conrad picked up his pace.

"Don't get me wrong," I said. "I believe you guys, but I'm having a hard time connecting the dots. I don't see why I'm some sort of missing link in this whole thing."

"We don't know the answer to that either," Conrad said, still focused on the path and on moving fast. "What we do know is that this opportunity may not come along again. It's time to take action."

If Conrad and the rest of Gateway were committed to me, then our interests were aligned. I wanted to save my son, and they wanted me to contribute to the effort to cripple PopCon before too much damage was done.

"So, what motivates you?" I asked Conrad. "Why are you so committed?"

"How much do you know about Monty?" A strange response to my question, but I decided to play along.

"We've become pretty close. Well, as close as people can get here."

"So, that means you know the story about his parents."

"Yes. Horrible. No kid should have to live through something like that."

"Well, and Monty doesn't know this, but he and I have a connection."

"You knew each other while you were alive?" I asked.

"No, but we knew some of the same people."

The terrain we were walking through was entirely different terrain than on my two previous trips across this space, but that was commonplace for me now. I barely noticed. What I wanted was for Conrad to get to the point.

"From Philly?" I asked him.

"Yes, from Philly."

"Come on, stop with the bullshit. Tell me the story."

"I didn't arrive here by mistake," Conrad said. He seemed to be enjoying this, but now his voice got stern. "Much like you, I have a purpose here."

"What's your purpose then?"

"I'm a natural enemy to Marshall, and that's why I'm here. My motivation to destroy him runs deep. Call it revenge." And at that point, shaking with emotion, Conrad shared the details of his reasons for hating Marshall.

Conrad, it turned out, was no angel. He had run with a rough crowd, often looking for shortcuts to money. These shortcuts were illegal and sometimes drew the ire of powerful men in the seedy underworld of Philadelphia. Conrad and his crew were considered dime store crooks. They would burglarize homes, steal cars, and rob convenience stores. Conrad was in jail for several short stints. He never got caught at anything major, but it was always enough to warrant jail time, and his rap sheet kept getting longer. On one of his stays behind bars, he met Marshall. Marshall was doing a twenty-eight month stint for battery on his son's mother. His big mistake here was that not only did he beat the woman, badly and in front of witnesses, but he did it while a restraining order was in effect. The judge tried to make his sentence longer, but he couldn't.

Marshall and Conrad bunked together for nine months. In that world, Conrad looked up to Marshall because he'd seen more, done

140

more, and knew many more important figures in the Philadelphia crime scene. Marshall might be a small-time gangster, but he was a professional criminal. Compared to him, Conrad was just a punk. The two of them spent twenty-three of the twenty-four hours of the day together. Conrad was Marshall's prison sidekick and, as such, he was protected. So, Conrad's stay was much easier than it would have been if Marshall hadn't taken the young man under his wing.

Marshall's crew on the outside still relied on him while he was in the lock up, but it was challenging. As his sentence went on, the influence he'd had on the outside began to dwindle. Marshall couldn't allow this to happen. He was a high-ranking guy outside the walls of the prison, and after his release he wanted to resume that position. It occurred to him that Conrad could be his lieutenant, his puppet-on-the-ground while Marshall pulled the strings from prison.

Conrad was due to be released in about four weeks. In those four weeks Marshall taught him everything about his crime ring. Marshall sent messages to the outside that Conrad would be his eyes and ears, and that Marshall expected the others to respect Conrad as they would respect Marshall. Conrad thought he hit the lottery. No more unorganized acts— no car boosting, convenience store stick-ups, or anything else. He was going to be part of the big time. He loved the idea of it.

Sure enough, after Conrad's release, he was treated with the same level of respect as Marshall. Acting on behalf of Marshall, Conrad had a voice in every deal that went down and took a significant piece of every transaction. The money was flowing in like never before. For the next twenty-one months, Conrad kept Marshall's seat warm while earning more than he had in all of the previous years of his life. He abandoned all of his old friends as he had nothing to gain by running with those petty thieves. The power and money were intoxicating, but Conrad's loyalty to Marshall ran deep. Conrad had no intention of supplanting his benefactor. His efforts were focused on maintaining Marshall's position. To Conrad, their relationship was that of a mentor and protégé.

Of course, loyalty is requisite in the underworld, but among gangsters, insecurity and paranoia are common. Crooks doubt allegiances and look over their shoulders at every turn, expecting the worst. It's a horrible way to live, but a livelihood that is hard to abandon once the money starts flowing. The guys who ran in Marshall's gang weren't equipped to quit their gangster lifestyles by taking corporate jobs. The dye had been cast for each of them, and turning back was impossible. Most either end up in prison or dead. Long term thinking is unheard of, which explains a lot of the rash decisions that were made on a regular basis. The sad part is that a lot of these guys aren't dumb. Maybe they're a bit lazy, but they're not stupid. Shortcuts are their thing. Why put in the time for a little reward? High risk, high reward, that's where it's at.

After Marshall was released, he resumed his role in the gang without complication. The only person that didn't think it was a seamless transition, inexplicably, was Marshall himself. His paranoia kicked in. He'd see Conrad cozying up to members of the group, and rather than commending him for a job well done, Marshall saw him as a threat. He didn't let on that he was jealous of Conrad. He kept his insecurities to himself, waiting for the right moment to end Conrad's position. Marshall didn't need a lieutenant now.

Marshall laid low for the first couple of months, knowing that the cops had an eye on him. As his comfort level began to rise, he immersed himself in all of the gang's plans. His opinions, ideas, and strategies were always respected. That didn't change. The latest project the gang was working on was to foil a drug deal between rival gangs, with the goal of ending up with both the money and the drugs scheduled to exchange hands that night. Marshall had an insider at each end of the transaction providing him with all of the details. He knew the meeting spot, how many members would be there, and the amount of money and drugs being exchanged. This ambush was risky, but that's how Marshall lived. He wasn't afraid of dying. The fear of dying was the downfall of many of the guys he ran with and against. That fear led to poor decision making. Marshall lived for the moment. On the outside he never thought ahead. The day he was alive was the day that he'd plan for. On the inside, he had to plan ahead. His scheme to place Conrad in an important role with the gang had worked, and now the time had come to end that association.

The Parkway Motel was often the scene of drug busts, prostitution stings, and many other failed endeavors. Marshall never did business there, and ridiculed the two rival gangs for picking this spot for their exchange. It was just another sign to Marshall that he was smarter than everyone else. These idiots were lazy. The Parkway was a convenient spot, not a safe one. The ambush would have to be quick and quiet as the cops were sure to pounce on the place as soon as any commotion arose. The two insiders had already met each other and knew exactly the time everything would go down. Eight men were scheduled to be in the tiny motel room. Three from one gang and five from the other. Two of the eight were in Marshall's back pocket, therefore, worst case scenario there'd be six men dead when the job was completed. Most men would shudder at the idea of executing six men in a matter of minutes, but Marshall saw it as a technical challenge.

The morning of the ambush Marshall summoned Conrad to his office. The big man talked about his desired outcome and the importance of moving swiftly. In his office a man named Sean sat in on the details. This struck Conrad as odd—he had neither met nor heard of Sean—but he trusted his mentor. The three of them plus the two insiders were to quickly dispose of the other six men. Marshall had a system for gunplay of this sort. Shoot to the right, that's how he explained it. Each man was right-handed, and the natural flow of shooting to the right provided for the best chance of kill shots. Each of the five guys in Marshall's gang were assigned one man each with the exception of the insider who had only two associates in attendance. He was responsible for taking them both out. He was instructed to position himself in the room to their left. The killing would occur in a counterclockwise fashion. This is how Marshall's mind worked. He was a nasty individual, but a brilliant gangster.

Marshall's distribution network was the distribution network in Philadelphia. Even rival gangs, such as the two they'd be ambushing, used this network for a percentage. So, this wasn't uncommon, and the rival gangs wouldn't be on guard. Marshall felt they'd be relaxed, and this gave him the opportunity to make a big score. He felt that his gang would ultimately do all of the work distributing and take most of the risk. Why should he settle for a small percentage when he could take the whole thing?

The meeting started out just like many of the meetings that Marshall had participated in. Some pleasantries ensued in a room clouded with cigarette smoke. Marshall didn't smoke at all and certainly wouldn't smoke during a transaction like this. His hands needed to remain free and ready. A relaxed gangster usually ends up as a dead gangster.

Two shots each, that's what it would take. Kill shots to the skull. Once Marshall laid his eyes on both the money and the drugs, he gave the signal. A tactic he had used before would prove to be successful again. With three groups in the motel together, he suggested they flip a coin to see who would take the floor first to list their negotiating points. Of course, most of the negotiating had been completed prior to the meet up, but a few loose ends always needed to be resolved. Marshall never flipped the coin. In this case, he had one of the soon-to-be-dead rival gangsters toss the coin into the air. While each of the six unsuspecting men watched the coin rise to the ceiling and drop to the bed, the shots began ringing out. Each of Marshall's men, as instructed, shot to their right. One, two then one, two, then one, two, then one, two, then one, two and finally, one, two. Six men lay lifeless on the floor in pools of blood. The plan's execution was flawless. The dead men never had a chance to take their guns out. Even the final man killed hadn't had time to defend himself. Sean and the two insiders gathered the drugs and money, which were in plain sight. Marshall motioned to Conrad to look under the bed to be sure they weren't leaving behind anything important. As Conrad bent down to lift up the bedspread, Sean blasted him in the back of the head. His brains spattered all over the bed, Conrad fell to the bloody floor. Marshall was the last to leave the dingy motel room. He closed the door behind him, and he and Sean carried away the big score.

So, it turned out that Conrad, who was dead, had never been a protégé. He was a puppet in Marshall's world—an instrument to be used then discarded. In Marshall's mind, his actions were proper and right. He had seen Conrad as a threat to his future. Never would he lose a minute of sleep over Conrad's demise. Now, these two men were navigating the afterlife, pitted against each other with a lot more at stake than drugs and money.

I had always feared Marshall, and Conrad's story served only to intensify that fear. My confidence that I could win against Marshall plummeted. I had survived our last encounter, but he had gotten to me, especially in the beginning. And hearing Conrad speak of his own demise had a negative impact on my mindset. Once again Marshall had the upper hand, and this time he'd gotten it without even confronting me. Just listening to Conrad's story had taken me ten steps back in my own progress. Even in death, Marshall was using Conrad as a puppet. This thought began to work in my mind.

"Conrad, I know this is going to sound extremely selfish, but can

I trust you? Or is Marshall still controlling you?"

"That's what you have to say? Really?" I guess Conrad expected some sympathy rather than doubt as a reaction to his heart-wrenching story.

"It's a fair question. It is," I stayed on point.

"I suppose you can trust me just as much as I can trust you, right?" He spoke without eye contact, still focused on the terrain in front of us.

"That makes sense." I paused. "So, no, I can't trust you!"

We both laughed. The reality of our situation was harsh, but to be expected under the circumstances.

CHAPTER EIGHTEEN

The path leading back to Gateway was littered with brush. We pushed our way through branches that scratched our calves, ankles, shins, and knees. This experience was yet another reminder of how odd this place was. Some of these scratches felt like a knife was slicing through me, but as usual, no blood was drawn. I felt that the terrain changes and the difficulties we had in navigating through them were trials placed before us—challenges to test our overall competence and mindset.

When I'd arrived in the afterworld, I'd often sit and rest in the process of moving from place to place. Not because I was physically tired, but because I felt mentally drained. I was past that now. There was a setback involving Marshall, but otherwise my mind has gotten consistently stronger in my time here. If someone were to ask me how long it had taken me to achieve this level, I'd have no idea how to answer. In the living person's timetable, it might have been years, months, days, or minutes. I had no way of knowing. No one in the afterworld was walking around with a watch. I had given up trying to count the sunrises and sunsets almost immediately. They didn't measure anything. The sun might be directly overhead, leading me to believe that it was about noon; then I'd walk a couple hundred steps and see the sun disappear behind the western horizon. I think one of the secrets of being in this realm is to forget everything you have learned about life. This isn't life. It's death, and death was never meant to be predictable.

Of course, neither was life. But when I was alive, I thought that I had some control, and that some natural, physical laws prevailed. The world I am in right now is not physical—and I seem to be at the whim of whatever is before me. Or behind me.

Conrad and I emerged from the brush. "Finally," I said. "That was brutal."

"I'll never understand it," Conrad said.

I assumed he was referring to the terrain. "Me neither, but at least we're out of it."

"No, that's not what I'm talking about. I'll never understand how I've arrived here." With a wave of his arm, Conrad took in our surroundings.

"I don't think it's ours to understand." This was the sum of my contemplation on the subject.

"That's fair. But still, don't you wonder: why us? There are so few of us here. Are you and I special, or are we being punished?"

"It's all up here," I tapped my index finger on my right temple.

"That's easy for you to say. You're strong minded and strong willed, a leader."

"You are, too, or you wouldn't be here." I tried to build his confidence.

"No," he said firmly. "I've never been much of anything. You heard my story. I was a loser while alive, and I'm quite certain I haven't changed."

I stopped in my tracks. We could see Gateway in the distance, only a couple hundred yards away.

"Stop being such a pussy, Conrad. We both have had it tough. We've both had our share of shitty moments, alive and dead. I don't have the patience to be on a team with someone who has such a negative mind set." That was harsh, but I felt I needed to say something strong in order to snap him back on track.

"That's what I get? You ungrateful bitch! Don't forget that I helped save you." With this, he stormed past me.

I knew where he was headed, but I wasn't concerned about his reaching Nathan and Nigel before me. I had spent too much of my life allowing others to drag me down with their negativity. Falling into a negative space is much easier than staying positive. People I knew who hated their jobs would consistently go to lunch with the same group of colleagues who also hated their jobs. They'd spend an hour bashing the company, their boss, their salaries… They'd go back to the office filled with negative thoughts, counting the minutes until five o'clock. They fed off of one another, never realizing the toxic environment that they had created. If one of these people ever chose to veer away from the lunch bunch, she was labeled a bitch. If she ever had something positive to say about anything company related, she was a brown-noser. This was the vicious cycle set in motion and it would usually end with a member of the group leaving the company for the greener grass only to end up bashing that company and taking down other employees in the process.

Negativity is ugly, and because it is such an easy place to get to, it can dominate a person's perspective—whether they're alive or dead. Conrad was letting his negativity control him, but I knew better than to let him take me down with him. I feel like I've made amazing progress here. There was a light at the end of the tunnel for me. I know that because I was almost there. "There" was undefined right now, but I understood that I'd know when I got to it. My current thoughts about "there" had me arriving in Heaven knowing that Ben was safe and free to live the life that he deserved. No one would be around to harm him. I was pretty sure that Cliff's body wouldn't see the outside of a jail cell again until it was being wheeled out on a gurney. My positive thinking will push me forward until my "there" is a reality.

The Gateway entrance was only about ten yards ahead. The doors swung open for Conrad, and he was greeted by a woman whom I had never seen before, which wasn't surprising. I'd only met Nathan and Nigel during my previous visit to Gateway.

"Hey, Izzy, thank you," Conrad said as he walked through the entrance. This woman then held the door open for me.

"Nathan would like to see you right away," the woman—Izzy, I guess—said to me, giving me no greeting and no smile. Still, I followed her. Izzy had black hair, pulled back into a tight ponytail. She was wearing a black jumper with a red belt, her ponytail almost reaching the top of the belt. She strutted, rather than walked, and her dark skin peaked out between her red heels and the bottom of her jumper.

Izzy and I arrived at a particular door, the only spot in Gateway that was familiar to me. I knew what was waiting for me beyond this door—another visit with Ben. Only this time I wouldn't be a spectator!

"I'll leave you here," Izzy told me. "Nathan will be with you shortly." Then she caught hold of my arm and gave it a squeeze. "Good luck, Maggie! We're praying for you." She smiled at me, before heading back toward the Gateway entrance.

"Hey, wait!" I called to her.

"Yes?" Izzy stopped and looked at me again. She seemed surprised that I was engaging in conversation with her.

"What do you know about this?"

"Oh, Maggie, we're all in this together. Everyone here has been eagerly awaiting your return. This is the best chance we've had since I came here." That was exactly what Conrad had said—and then I realized that Conrad had quietly disappeared.

"Please do me a favor," I said. "If you see Conrad, let him know I'm sorry. I was a bit harsh with him earlier."

"He'll be fine. He did a great job delivering you, and that's what he should be focused on." Izzy turned, ending our conversation just as I heard the door behind me slowly open.

Nigel walked out with both arms outstretched, looking as though he wanted to give me a hug. I cut him off, taking both of his hands in mine. This wasn't a couple of friends about to catch up on old times. I saw this as a business meeting. I still don't know much about Gateway, but they were treating me like I was some kind of savior. There was only one person I'd met in the afterworld whom I still trusted—Monty. I so wished Monty was with me now. I could use a second opinion on all of this.

"Maggie, you're back. Wonderful to see you!" Nigel didn't get the hint that a hug was not in the cards, and he leaned in close—a move I rebuffed by backing up.

"Where's Nathan?" I didn't want small talk.

"Aren't you the anxious one!"

Nigel's attempt at humor misfired and set me off. I raised my voice, crying out, "Stop this already." My words echoed down the hallway.

"Lower your voice," Nigel demanded, in an annoying whisper.

I didn't. "Why? Are we in church?"

"That's enough!" Nigel grabbed my wrist and started pulling me toward the door.

That did it for me. "Get off me!" I was yelling, and I pried my arm free.

Nathan appeared in the doorway then, the picture of calm. He asked, "What's going on out here?"

"Tell your lackey to keep his Goddamned hands off me," I yelled, glaring at Nigel.

"Nigel, go." Nathan made a dismissive motion to Nigel, and Nigel walked down the hallway in the same direction Izzy had taken.

I entered the room then and saw the familiar pod. I really wanted to get this over with. I think yelling at Nigel was just a way for me to get across that I was a bit on edge. In the past when I felt like this, I would have thought my period was on the way. But there's no such thing now—one of the many benefits of being dead.

"Please have a seat," Nathan motioned to the head of the conference table as he sat down in one of the other seats.

Why was I at the head of the table? I asked him, "What have you told all of these people?" I could feel the energy in the building, the mounting pressure. Too much was riding on my visit to Ben!

"We are an open book here," Nathan said in his easygoing voice. "It helps to garner positive energy. We've all been praying for your safe return, and now our prayers continue as you get ready to visit Ben." It seemed he was saying that I was, indeed, their savior.

"Aren't you all getting a bit ahead of yourselves?" I had always preferred the approach of under promise and over deliver.

"We have confidence in you, Maggie." Nathan leaned in and looked me square in the eye. "You're going to do this well."

He got up from his chair and walked to the door.

"I'm going to leave you for a bit. I'll be back soon. Please relax. We're all here for you." Nathan left, closing the door behind him.

I was supposed to feel supported and confident, but this whole thing was creeping me out. Gateway felt like a cult. Everyone had a glazed look in their eyes. So, what was I doing here? As far as I knew, Gateway housed the only portal to the living. Saving my one living son from the demonic Marshall was my goal, and if this helped others in the process, that   was fine by me.

And Nathan was absolutely right: I needed to relax. Right now, I was in no shape to make this trip to save Ben. The pressure placed on me by all of Gateway was unfair—but it was the pressure I'd been placing on myself that was almost too much to bear. I had done a lot of yoga while I was alive, and I'd always found breathing exercises to be the most efficient way to calm my nerves. I took a seat on the floor with my legs crossed and my hands on my knees, and I started breathing in through my nose and out through my mouth. Breathing deeply, breathing slowly. I could feel my heart rate begin to drop. Hopefully, this meditation would get me to the mental place I needed to be in to make a smooth trip to save Ben. If I could calm myself, the only thing that would be missing was a plan.

Just the thought of the word "plan" made me nervous. My heart rate began pounding faster, and so I focused again on my breathing. After a few more deep breaths, I felt better—but I was still without a plan. I mused that I hadn't followed a plan yet, and still I had come this far. I've never been the type to "wing it," but that seems to be what this place was about. I would get myself mentally ready, and then I'd have to proceed from there. This was for Ben, my baby boy. Ben needed his momma, more than he ever had. I was going to make it happen.

I rose to my feet and walked to the other side of the room. As I walked by glass that bordered the far wall, I could see my reflection. I had learned that appearances here didn't mean much, but it was difficult not to be startled by the image I found looking back at me. I was an old woman. My face was wrinkled and dotted with liver spots. If I'd been asked to guess my age, I'd have said late eighties. I smiled and thought, now you know what you would've looked like if you'd lived that long. I didn't have any complaints. It wasn't too bad for an old lady. I glanced down to my hands. While the reflection showed an arthritic hand with bent knuckles, the hand on my body appeared to be much younger. Not the teenage me but perhaps me in my forties. Just another strange occurrence in this place that produces more strange than normal.

The door opened, and Nathan and Nigel came in. I know they weren't trying to pressure me to begin my journey, but I too felt the weight of what was ahead. There was no reason to wait any longer.

"OK, let's do this." I walked over to the pod.

"Yes, let's do it," Nathan said with a smile that showed no teeth.

I had always thought it odd when people smiled without showing their teeth—unless, of course, they had a physical issue they were trying to hide. Nathan had no issues with his teeth; it was just his way. It was the one oddity that made me doubt him, but it didn't matter now. Ben was my responsibility, and Gateway had the only vehicle that connected the afterlife to the living. These guys had the monopoly on this pathway, and this would be my second time taking advantage of it. As far as I knew, never before had anyone been given the opportunity to make two trips. Suddenly, I had a question I felt I had to ask.

"Why have you both placed so much trust in me?"

Nathan didn't hesitate in his reply. "Opportunities like this are rare. On the one hand, we have faith in you, and on the other, we don't have much of a choice. I'm not sure if that's the answer you're looking for, but we've prepared for a person like you to come into our world, and now that you have, we're ready to assist you in any way possible."

This was an answer I could trust. I placed my left hand on the upper portion of the pod, my right leg on the bottom portion, and pushed my way up and over into the seating area. I was still amazed at how simple the pod was. You might have thought it would look like an airplane cockpit with lots of gadgets and instruments, but it was nothing of the sort. It was a place to set my mind at ease as it guided me to my destination.

"Good luck, Maggie! We'll be praying for you." Nathan gently touched my forearm, and then he and Nigel left the room.

The door shut, and the lights dimmed. A cold rush pushed through the room, but this had little impact on me. If anything, it allowed me to concentrate more on what I was doing. A light buzzing sound started, and this created a sense of flow, pushing me deeper into my meditation. This journey would be different from the last for several reasons—the primary being that this time I had a goal in mind. Last time I had been a voyager; now I was a warrior—now I had a result in mind.

My eyes remained closed as my arms melted into my sides. I felt a floating sensation, much like I was in a body of densely salted water. I gently moved my feet and felt the slight resistance in the atmosphere. I moved my arms and felt resistance there as well. A brief burst of brightness pierced my eyelids. I opened my eyes and saw that I had arrived.

To my surprise, what I saw was familiar. I was in my own home rather than Lisa's. The feeling in my hands and feet returned, and my bare feet landed on the wood floor in our living room. Sitting on the mantle over the fireplace was a photo of our family, but not a recent photo. I remember that scene like it was yesterday. I was about eight months pregnant with Reese. The boys were eight, five, and three. I vividly remember the photo because it had been almost impossible to get the boys settled and smiling in unison. By the time we got home that day,

I was exhausted from battling with the three of them while carrying all of that extra weight.

The photo turned out to be beautiful, however, and I'd placed it on the mantle two days before Reese was born. I hadn't seen it in a long time, as each year we'd take another photograph to replace the one on the mantle. I should have made more of an effort to reminisce with the boys. Sure, they may not have enjoyed it at the time, but I bet they would have appreciated it later. I don't know where any of those photos are now. I hope Ben received them. It might be hard for him to look at them right now, but hopefully after a few years, his memories of the good times will overshadow the bad.

I broke my trance and moved into the hallway leading to the kitchen. A mirror hung in the hallway, and I caught my reflection. Once again, my appearance had changed. I was exactly the woman in the photo on the mantle. The mirror only reflected my image from about my chest up, but it was spot on. I looked downward to see if the reflection matched the actual view, and what I saw startled me. I was pregnant. I placed my hands on my belly as I so often did during all of my pregnancies. My left hand was underneath my belly while the right was on top. Reese started kicking. I felt the sensation just as if it were actually happening. Cliff and I loved placing our hands on my belly and feeling the kids' kicks. We always told each of them how excited we were and that we couldn't wait to see them. Cliff would kiss my belly and place his cheek on it for a few moments. Those moments were so sweet. He was in his own little world then, with his eyes closed and a little grin on his face. These kids meant the world to him. I'll never understand why he did what he did, but if there was ever a chance of my finding the answers, I was in the right place to do it.

Reese continued to kick. I pulled up my dress to get a better view. She was really going at it, much like she did when I was actually pregnant. I placed my right hand back on the top of my belly. As I placed it the kicking stopped. I was astonished to see a perfect fluorescent green outline of my hand shine from underneath my skin. It was the identical shade of green that I'd seen on the path to PopCon, and once again, it was pulsing like a heartbeat. I brought my left hand up from under my belly and placed it on top, next to my right hand. The fluorescent green outline appeared as well. Both hands were now pulsing in the exact same rhythm. I'd be foolish to think that this wasn't related to what I witnessed on the path. But I didn't know how or why, and neither experience had provided any clues.

The wood floor behind me creaked. I spun around removing my hands from my belly and dropping my dress down. The fluorescent green pulsing subsided, and again I felt Reese kicking. My eyes had trouble focusing, but when I zeroed in on the figure before me, I almost fell to the ground in astonishment. There he was, eight-year-old Ben.

"Mom, I can't sleep," he said, looking right at me, standing only three feet away.

My instinct was to look over my shoulder as he couldn't be speaking to me.

"Mom?" He didn't understand why I wasn't responding, and he took a step closer.

"Ben?" I said as if I was meeting him for the first time.

"Are you OK? You're acting funny."

"Yes, honey, I'm fine." I quickly got into character.

He took another step closer and clutched my hand. The fluorescent green pulsing started up again between our two hands.

"Ben, do you see that?" I asked, referring to the pulsing green.

"Huh?" He pulled me toward the kitchen without a mention of the vivid glow emanating from our hands.

I looked up at the clock in the kitchen, it was 11:45 p.m. During all of my pregnancies I found myself getting up in the middle of the night due to general discomfort, but these little trips would also allow the blood to flow a little better. Sometimes Cliff would join me in the kitchen or one of the kids. Since Ben was the oldest, he and I had spent a lot of time together over glasses of milk. I'd stand, and he'd sit. He did this so often during Reese's pregnancy that I knew he was doing it on purpose. He'd wait until he heard me walking down the hall and then make his way out of his room to spend time with me. It was extremely sweet, and it got to be so that I expected him to come. I'd be disappointed if he didn't join me. It was our time away from the everyday chaos that a family of five, soon to be six, can produce.

Ben would share things with me during those late-night talks that never saw the light of day. Some were trivial, but others were pretty deep for an eight-year-old. He had an odd fascination with death and asked a lot of questions about dying and what happened afterward. We'd recently had a run of deaths in our family involving some of the older aunts and

154

uncles on both my side and Cliff's. Ben was old enough to comprehend death, but he didn't have a real grasp of what it was, which wasn't surprising. Most of his fascination was focused on where people went after they passed on. He'd attend a funeral and then leave it with more questions than answers. Rather than ask Cliff those questions, Ben used our late-night talks as an opportunity to explore the intricacies of life and death. Of course, I now found these conversations eerily ironic. My answers at the time were based on what I knew—or thought I knew. Clearly, I knew nothing, but neither did anyone else. I shared what I had thought—"knowledge" that I had no reason to doubt.

"Do you want me to warm it up for you?" The refrigerator was open. I had a glass in one hand and a gallon of milk in the other.

"Yes, please." Ben always liked his milk warmed up. I'm not sure why I bothered asking. I suppose my mind hadn't yet focused on this strange encounter. It was easy for me to think that his preferences may have changed since it had been so long since we'd last sat in the kitchen for one of these conversations.

"Here you go." I placed the warm glass on the placemat in front of him. He grabbed it with both hands, bringing it to his lips. After a big gulp the usual milk mustache remained, which always brought a smile to both of our faces.

"Thank you." Ben took another gulp. The glass was less than half full after only two drinks from it.

I knew I was here for a reason, but I let myself get lost in the moment. I was kicking myself now because, while I'd enjoyed these special times with Ben, I hadn't thought about them since. Once Reese was born, these special moments with Ben had ceased. I'd never asked him how that had made him feel or if he experienced a void without them. I should have been more considerate. It was clear how much these talks had meant to him. After all, he'd purposely wait up until he heard me in the hallway. He'd act like he had just woken up. But after a while, we both knew better. It was our little secret, although Cliff would crash our little parties every now and then. Ben and I didn't mind, as long as Cliff's visits were kept to a minimum.

"I'm sorry, Ben." The words just slipped out of my mouth.

"What?" How could he respond with anything but a question?

I left the kitchen as my eyes began to well up. The gravity of the situation hit me. I had gotten absorbed into the moment like I had gone back in time. When I realized the actual circumstances, I'd lost my composure.

"Mom, where are you going?"

"Hold on, Benny. I'll be right back." I found myself standing in front of the mirror in the hallway again.

Silently, tears began to flow down my cheeks. It took everything in me to stay quiet as I didn't want Ben to see me like this. I placed both of my hands on my belly again, this time outside of my dress. I expected to see the same fluorescent green pulsing, but nothing happened. I felt a tear trying to escape at the end of my chin. It left my face as I looked downward to my hands. In slow motion, the tear fell, landing on my hand, where it flashed fluorescent green. Another tear followed, hitting my other hand and doing the same thing. I lifted both hands from my belly, and the green disappeared as the tears rolled down my wrists and blended in with my skin. I had stood here in awe long enough.

"Ben?" I whispered as I turned and went back into the kitchen.

"Yes." The voice was Ben's, but he no longer sounded like an eight-year-old child.

I braced myself for what was waiting around the corner. There he was sitting at the table: the same Ben I had seen for the last time that fateful night in July. My seventeen-year-old son was sitting in front of me with a half full glass of warm milk.

"I wish we could be a family again," Ben said. I began to think that all of this was just in my mind. I wondered if I was simply hallucinating. But I decided to trust what was happening, whatever it was. I took a deep breath before responding.

"What do you see, Ben?" I asked this because I needed to know how Ben perceived me.

He was looking at me, or at least I thought he was. His line of sight seemed slightly off to my left.

"You know what she's doing, don't you?" Ben asked.

I was confused by the question. Before I could answer, I felt a presence on my left side.

It was Cliff. He said, "I'm not dumb, Ben. I'm not."

This startled me—not because of Cliff's presence in the room, but because I knew I was witnessing a conversation that had taken place about me and my infidelities. Here I was, caught in the middle of a conversation about me with no ability to respond or even try to defend myself.

"Then why don't you confront her? This is embarrassing. Do you know how many people know about this?" Ben's fingers stroked the glass of milk before taking another gulp.

"I don't know how to," Cliff said.

"What do you mean you don't know how to?" Ben raised his voice.

"Just calm down. You'll wake everyone up." Cliff quickly stepped closer to Ben, taking the seat next to him.

"Don't you guys still love each other?"

"I'll never stop loving your mom, but it might just be too late for us." Cliff clenched his fist.

"I don't know how you can sit back and take this. Look what she's doing. Look what she's doing to our family. It's not fair!" It seemed to me that Ben sounded more adult than Cliff in this conversation.

"You'll learn someday, pal. You'll learn that it's not so easy raising a family and keeping a marriage together." Cliff stood up.

"Where are you going?" Ben's voice rose again.

"I don't need to be interrogated by my own son." Cliff walked away, seeming to pass right through my body and into the hallway.

Ben's right hand backhanded the milk glass, sending it into the kitchen wall, where it shattered. The milk was gone, but the glass was aplenty. He went to his room, leaving the mess behind. I walked over to the kitchen counter and out of habit attempted to grab the paper towels in an effort to clean up the glass. That simple task was not possible. I couldn't impact anything in the room in the way I had previously, when conversing with the eight-year-old Ben.

The calendar on the refrigerator was the kind where each day had a motivational statement or quote from a famous figure, either past or present. The date on the calendar read July 24, 2016, which was just two days before the murders. That day's quote was from Mark Twain: "I do not fear death. I had been dead for billions and billions of years before I was born, and had not suffered the slightest inconvenience from it."

I was always the one in the family to update the calendar each morning. Sometimes I'd read the quote to the family as everyone gathered in the morning for breakfast. I don't ever remember reading this one. I don't even remember tearing away July 23 from the calendar. There was good reason for that. I was hungover on the morning of July

24, following my night out with Brent. We had gotten sloppy, and our infidelities were no longer a secret to Cliff. What I hadn't realized until this moment was that Ben was aware of them as well. What a terrible role model I had been for Ben. I had become an embarrassment for him.

When I had arrived home that night, Cliff appeared to be sleeping, but I bet that was just his way of keeping everything bottled up inside. I took a shower and then lay in bed right next to the man I was cheating on. The man who had been nothing but caring and loving to me and our children. I was still drunk, and I'm sure I reeked of alcohol even after my shower. Looking back, I was surprised he hadn't killed me that night.

Cliff got up the next morning at his usual time. He sat in the kitchen as each kid, one by one, woke up and got ready for church. While nursing my hangover, I stupidly convinced myself that I'd be in the clear and a crisis would be averted. I had no idea that my infidelity would be a topic of conversation between my husband and our eldest son, who sat at the kitchen table and talked about me the next night while I slept.

I stood in the kitchen alone and in silence. I had come here with the intention of saving Ben, but other than my brief interaction with him, I hadn't accomplished anything. My mental focus began to fade. The room grew cold, signaling the end of my time here. My eyes opened and I was back at Gateway. Nathan and Nigel had not entered the room yet. I knew they'd be disappointed in me, but not as disappointed as I was in myself. I was disappointed that I hadn't garnered any helpful knowledge from this trip.

Besides, witnessing the conversation between Cliff and Ben hit me hard. A seventeen-year-old shouldn't have to go through what I had put him through. It was bad enough that Cliff had experienced what I put him through, but he was a grown man and better equipped to handle it. At Ben's age, he may be mature enough to understand the intricacies of affairs and infidelities, but how could he possibly grasp the many details that lead to a marriage falling apart! It was clear that I failed him as a mother, and that was something that I'd carry with me forever.

I used to think that "forever" ended when a person died, and that everything would be made right by passing through to the other side. That Mark Twain quote on the refrigerator calendar made all the sense in the world now. Life is just a simple pause, a brief period. What happens before we are born and after we die is what fills our souls. The life I thought I was living lasted a mere forty-four years. That timeframe equated to a blink of the eye here. Life might present many challenges, but nothing could compare to the afterlife.

Nathan and Nigel entered the room, eagerly anticipating a download from me. Their body language and overall demeanor clearly showed me how much this trip meant to them, making it that much more difficult to share my failure with them.

"How are you feeling?" Nathan bent down on one knee next to me as I still lay in the pod.

"I'm tired, Nathan. My mind has been beaten to hell." The exhaustion I was experiencing was like no other time in the afterlife.

"Understandable," Nigel chimed in. He was standing behind Nathan's right shoulder.

"What did you learn?" Nathan asked.

I pushed myself up and out of the pod, straightened my dress, and set my bare feet on the cold floor. Not only had I come back with nothing, but I'd also solidified the fact that I had been a horrible wife and mother. My patience was running thin. The last thing I wanted right now was to be questioned by these two.

"Do you really want to know what I learned?" I asked in a level tone.

"Of course we do," Nathan replied.

"I'll tell you what I learned. I learned that I was a shitty mother. I learned that I was an unfaithful, selfish wife. I learned that my family's murder was the direct result of my selfish acts. I learned that I have no power or capacity to save my son." My voice rose as I went through this litany. By the end, I was shaking.

Nathan and Nigel seemed stunned. They had seen me upset before, but now I was apparently on the verge of a breakdown. Once again, just when I'd thought I had something figured out, I had been shown how little I knew and just how insignificant I was in the grand scheme of things.

I was leaning against the wall and allowed myself to slowly slide my back down the wall until I was leaning against it, seated on the floor. I held my head in my hands, and a few tears dropped to the floor between my legs. "I have nothing else to give you," I said, finally looking up at them.

"There must have been something," Nathan pleaded. "Try to remember, please."

Remembering was not my problem. I wanted to forget what I'd witnessed, but that was impossible. So, I decided to share every detail with the two of them, even if it meant rehashing the entire painful experience. I told them about the eight-year-old Ben, the odd fluorescent glowing on my pregnant belly, and the conversation I had witnessed between Cliff and seventeen-year-old Ben. I gave them a complete download, not holding back one detail.

They were both desperate for any positive information and grasped onto the glowing and fluorescent green. Conrad had told them about the similar glowing that we'd seen on the path to PopCon. Clearly, there was a relationship between the two, but uncovering why and what the relationship meant would take additional effort.

Once again, making this effort fell on me.

"It's time for you to go back to that path," Nathan told me. "Answers are there; I'm sure of it." I could see that Nathan was a silver lining kind of guy. I saw problems; he saw opportunity in the problems.

My first instinct was to fight back on this notion that I should return to the path, but I refrained. I had been beaten down mentally. I was too weak to fight anything right now. It was easier for me to agree with them, especially since it meant that I could get out of here.

"That's fine," I said. "Just give me some time to re-energize." I thought about that for a second before adding, "Actually, forget about that. I'm ready now."

I didn't care anymore. No, I wasn't giving up, but my attitude sucked. I wanted this to end somehow, some way. Any way. I had lost track of my storybook ending, and now my only concern was getting to an ending. It's a dangerous mindset, but it's where I was.

CHAPTER NINETEEN

This journey reminded me of my friend Julia and her battle with breast cancer. Our kids' activities had brought us together, and her breast cancer eventually drove us apart. I had experienced more pain in this friendship than with anything else in my life—with anything else until I arrived in the afterworld. Julia and I had been best friends, and I was by her side through the few peaks and the many valleys that her diagnosis brought with it. Many women had successfully beaten breast cancer, and I was confident that Julia would have her own success story. When she was diagnosed, I was the first person she contacted. She needed advice on how to break the news to her husband and, eventually, her nine   and twelve-year-old girls. I had no experience with anything of such magnitude, but I'd done my best to assist her. I was with her for her appointments and treatments, I picked her kids up when she couldn't, and I helped with anything else that I could.

When Julia was diagnosed, her cancer was already advanced— stage three. While we hoped she would respond favorably to the various treatments, she didn't, and the cancer progressed. Before long, Julia was at stage four. Even those with the most positive of attitudes eventually are forced to face reality. That's what happened with Julia. She had been an amazing exemplar of hope and positivity for everyone whose life she'd touched. She always put on a happy face when interacting with her daughters and her husband, David. She didn't want them to remember her for anything but happiness. Because of her efforts to shield the three of them from the pain she was going through, I became a natural outlet for my friend. While I was OK with playing this role, there were times when it was excruciating. I understood that I was there to listen, but my natural instinct was to try to provide answers and solutions. As the cancer took over, I became helpless.

I remember the moment like it was yesterday. It was a Friday, June 8, 2010, to be exact. I had become obsessed with Julia's plight and ignored my own responsibilities in order to be by her side as much as possible. Cliff, being the ever-supportive husband, allowed me to stray from my own family so that I could help my friend in need. I arrived at the hospital around 6:00 p.m. Julia and I briefly joked about how we enjoyed our Friday evening happy hours prior to her getting sick much more than we did right now. Our conversation quickly turned from light-hearted to serious. After I had done my usual tidying up for her in the room, I sat down in my chair next to her bed. I brought her a couple of People magazines from which I'd typically read a few of the stories. She loved celebrity gossip.

I started to read one of the stories, but she interrupted me. I looked into her eyes and knew something wasn't right. "My fight is over," she said. It wasn't just because the doctors were telling her so; more importantly, she knew this herself.

I had never wanted to hear Julia admit defeat, and, at first, I didn't accept it. I told her she would be OK, that she'd fight back—the old down-but-not-out message. Julia was firm though. She'd had enough, and she was too tired to keep fighting. She felt it was time to accept her fate, and so she did.

Two days later I witnessed Julia taking her last breath. David and I held her hands as she drifted off. She was at peace, and sometimes that is the hardest part, the simple acceptance of death. The two days that she'd remained on Earth after her acceptance of dying were different from any other days since her diagnosis—any other days in her whole life, as far as I could tell. She was relieved, and it showed. She had resisted accepting her fate for fear that she would be looked down upon by everyone, that she'd be seen as a coward, as someone who gave up. But Julia hadn't given up at all. She'd broken free.

Now, I had a challenge ahead of me. Just like Julia, I wasn't giving up. I was marching forward, for better or for worse. PopCon had been hanging around my neck like a noose. Anticipation and fear of the unknown had dictated my every move in the afterworld, but that period was over. It was time for me to break free.

I opened the door to find Nathan, Nigel, and Conrad all patiently waiting for me in the hallway.

"Conrad's going to join you," Nathan said.

"Fair enough." I liked Conrad. He had proven to be quite capable. Having him by my side would be helpful.

The four of us walked to the front of Gateway. Once again, I'd be leaving here, but this time my plan was solid. I was going to PopCon and no place else. I had tried to save Ben using Gateway's resources, but that hadn't worked. His fate rested on my shoulders now, and that's how I wanted it to be. I'd be controlling my own destiny rather than relying on others.

"Good luck, and God bless you both." Nathan took my right hand and Conrad's left.

As the two of us left the building, I felt sure I'd never see Nathan or Nigel again. Not because they'd be gone, but because I would. I would take care of my business at PopCon and then, hopefully, I'd   be placed next to my children in Heaven.

"Looks like it's you and me again," I said to Conrad as we made our way over the now familiar path.

"Yep, I guess so." He wasn't as enthused as I was, but that wasn't surprising after our last encounter.

"You're not over it yet?" I said, sounding like Cliff when he'd insist that I get over some spat we had.

"Nope." Conrad kept walking.

"Yeah, I bet you'll get over it. Give it some time, right?" My light laughter was not returned.

In the short time that we've known each other, Conrad and I had developed an odd relationship. Sometimes it was difficult to figure out who was helping who. He was more of a follower than he was a leader, and I was OK with that. Every leader needs good soldiers for support. My demeanor and overall confidence had changed drastically since I arrived. I knew exactly what I wanted and felt that I had a decent plan to get it. I didn't need Conrad to join me on this journey, but I was pretty sure that he needed me. The only one I'd grown to rely on while I'd been here was Monty. I was Monty's soldier.

"This is it for you, isn't it?" Conrad said, ending the silent treatment.

"As a matter of fact, it is."

"How do you know that?"

"I suppose I don't, but it really doesn't matter. I won't be back at Gateway," I shared this information with Conrad without worry. Any potential consequences with Nathan didn't concern me.

"You've progressed rapidly." Conrad piqued my interest with this observation.

"What do you mean?"

"I mean I've never seen someone like you, and I've seen a lot of souls pass through here."

"I'm not sure what to think of that comment. I've been told that before, and it wasn't meant in any positive way. To sum it up, you're saying that I'm a bitch." I had to laugh.

"No, you've got it all wrong." Conrad smiled as he tried to explain what he'd meant. "Well, you've got most of it wrong, anyway."

"That's OK. You can say it. Nothing like that bothers me anymore." I wanted him to be candid.

Conrad walked in silence for about ten steps before he got up the courage to share his thoughts.

"Maggie, you're here for a much greater purpose. It's not a coincidence. I've seen many souls come and go. They jump into the Memory Pool and are never seen or heard from again. Or they arrive at the path and end up at PopCon, forced to spend eternity doling out punishments that they have no say in delivering."

My knowledge was limited regarding the Path of Lost Souls, and I had thought the name meant just that: they were lost. Conrad was implying that something else happened to them, something beyond their control.

"What do you mean 'doling out punishments?'"

"Just that. They are the conduit between PopCon and the living, but they come in sheep's clothing."

We were just about halfway to Vulture Point when Conrad began telling me about his personal encounter with PopCon. As I listened to his story, I began to understand Gateway's interest in me and why my role here might be so pivotal to both the living and the dead.

Just as I had, Conrad entered the afterworld at Vulture Point. He then jumped into the Memory Pool, hand in hand with a man named Constantine. Constantine had been the soul responsible for shepherding those arriving at Vulture Point prior to Monty. Conrad successfully navigated the waters of the Memory Pool, finding his way to the Path of Lost Souls. His attempts to enter Heaven had been rejected and that's where the similarities of our stories ended. His path led him into the hands of Joanna.

Joanna was the true wolf in sheep's clothing. She encountered souls when they felt all hope had been lost. They were at their lowest. Most had been rejected at the doors to Heaven and were left without answers or a plan to move forward. To say that they were vulnerable is an understatement. Joanna would use this disappointment to her advantage, shepherding souls away from their families and friends who were waiting for them in Heaven. Instead, she convinced them that PopCon held all of the answers, not only for them but also for the loved ones they'd left behind—the loved ones who were still alive. She'd sell PopCon as the opportunity to play God and, thus, to protect those they cared about.

Not everything Joanna shared was a lie. Those that are accepted into the PopCon community have some control over the fate of their loved ones, but not in the way they'd been told they would have. Nothing about life or the living would come out of PopCon. PopCon was all about the demise of the human spirit. Sometimes this demise would be peaceful; at other times it's violent. Being a part of the PopCon community could give a soul the power to impact the way in which their loved ones died, but never allowed any kind of avoidance. Death is inevitable for all of the living; it's only the way death comes to an individual that can be variable.

Not everyone arriving at PopCon was automatically accepted into the community, and once someone is accepted, it's rare that person would leave. Conrad was one of the exceptions.

"I beat them with my mind," Conrad tapped his temple with an index finger.

"What does that mean?"

"You know, Maggie, it's all up here." He continued to tap his temple, and he smiled.

"But how did you beat them?"

"I didn't let them steal my soul, that's how." Conrad lowered his hand from his temple to his heart.

As he continued to speak about what had happened to him, my confidence that I could successfully confront PopCon increased. What Conrad had done was not allow PopCon to enter his mind. I've been challenged often here, and I've withstood an onslaught of mental torment. I knew I was now stronger because of it.

"That's why you're here: your mind." He pointed at me then, directing his finger between my eyes.

"Why are you telling me this now? Why didn't you share this with me at Gateway?"

Conrad smiled. "You'll have to ask Nathan that question. I'm not supposed to be telling you now, but I see something in you that I think can save us all. That's why I'm telling you now. Gateway won't like it, but I don't care. I've started to doubt their capabilities. Look at how they handled the situation with you. It was horrible."

I wouldn't classify Conrad as a traitor, but if Nathan or Nigel heard him right now, they might think differently. Sometimes a little dissension in the ranks is healthy. I had my own opinions of Gateway, and they weren't entirely flattering. They seemed to do more talking than doing, and that's never been my style. I suppose that's why I'm out here with Conrad now.

"Joanna despises me, and that makes me smile," Conrad said—and he was smiling. "I beat her. No one else has beaten her like I did."

I began to feel at ease with Conrad as I had with Monty. I told him, "I think our paths have crossed for a reason."

"Nothing here happens by coincidence."

So, I finally had a teammate in this battle. It was invigorating. "OK, how do we beat them?"

"I have my thoughts," Conrad said, "but we won't really know how to beat them until we have the opportunity to do it." This was a chicken-or-egg kind of logic that didn't make much sense to me.

"What does that mean?"

"It means that we have to be nimble and react appropriately when we're in our confrontation with them. There is no playbook on this because it's never been done before." Conrad spoke with a confidence that I found both surprising and inspiring.

"Revenge is powerful," I added. "And Marshall will soon feel just how powerful it is."

Conrad stopped walking and spun me around until we were eye-to-eye. "No, Maggie," he said. "That is exactly how we fail."

"What do you mean?" I tried to pull away, but his grip tightened. Was he saying I was wrong? "But we have to settle the score with Marshall!"

"That's what you want? Revenge?"

"Yes! Of course! Don't you?" I kept pulling away, but Conrad was not letting me go.

"If anyone should want revenge against Marshall, it's me," he said. "But no. I don't want revenge. What I want is to get to Heaven. That's my motivation."

Conrad let go of my hands then, and I stood still, continuing to look into his eyes. His statement was brief, but powerful. Because it was true. It was also true for me. Neither one of us needed any kind of revenge. We were here for salvation.

Somehow, I had become obsessed with Marshall. My maternal instinct to protect my son had taken over, and defeating Marshall had become all I thought about. Conrad was putting it all into perspective. Nothing we did here was temporary. The consequences would last forever. If I actually made it to Heaven, I don't think I would ever forget what had happened here, in the afterlife. Hopefully, it would make me a better person, a better mother to my children. But I'm a bit envious of those who pass straight through. They'd successfully avoided this place, and I wonder if they weren't better for it. No one should have to experience what I'd experienced, including Marshall. Just like me, he was here for a reason. Perhaps I should pray for him.

"Once we arrive at Vulture Point, we should take a break," Conrad said. I looked at him again and realized that he was tired.

"I never thought I'd miss sleeping like I do right now," I told him. I closed my eyes and imagined cuddling up in my bed on a cold, rainy day with everything tucked in under my blankets except for my head.

We smiled at each other. "It's really quite unfair, isn't it?" Conrad said. "Would you have ever thought that you'd be exhausted but unable to sleep?"

"I guess sleep is for the living." It was a simple but accurate statement.

"Who'd have thought that being dead would be so fatiguing?" Conrad said, and we both laughed at our odd predicament.

CHAPTER TWENTY

Before we knew it, Conrad and I had arrived at Vulture Point. Monty was nowhere in sight. Selfishly, I wanted to see him again, and unselfishly, I hoped that he had crossed over. I have faith that we'll be reunited, but it won't be here. We both deserve to make it to Heaven. That would be an amazing reunion if it happened.

Conrad and I decided to sit for a moment at the circle where Monty had originally drawn me a map of this weird place. The drawing was gone, of course.

I scanned the area and said, "It's hard to appreciate the beauty of this place, but just look around. It's extraordinary."

"It's easy to mistake this place for Heaven," Conrad said, "as long as you're only looking at it." For a moment we both watched the sun dip lower and lower to the west.

"Looks like Heaven, and feels like Hell," I said, and Conrad gave me a nod of agreement.

The sun disappeared, allowing for the moon and stars to take over and provide their own mellow light. Conrad and I purposely didn't say much to one another because, for each of us, getting our mind right was our number one priority. The night came, and then it ended—giving no sense of the passage of time. Several times in the past I had tried to count aloud to show the passage of time in my head. I wanted to see what an hour looked like. I'd failed every time. There was no clock here. This was just one more reminder of how vulnerable we were to the whims of whatever forces were in control here. It was a terrible scenario for an OCD control freak like me. Oh well, I would just need to pay attention to my own mental state.

When I felt confident, I turned to Conrad. "Ready?" I asked.

"Yep." His confidence seemed high as well.

I think we had both arrived at a place in our minds where we

168

simply didn't care anymore. When you have nothing, you have nothing to lose.

"We need to get back to that path with the glowing rocks," I said. "That's our way to PopCon." I was saying this as if it were fact, but it is where I thought we should begin.

"I hope we can find it." Conrad knew that the inconsistency of the terrain might make it challenging to locate.

"Follow our gut," I said. "That's what we'll need to do. We'll get there, and then I'm going to save my boy." I knew this was my last chance.

I remembered that the glowing path was just southeast of the Memory Pool. I wasn't thrilled about going anywhere near the Memory Pool, but it seemed the best tactic for finding our way.

"I fucking hate that pool," I said when we were just to the east of it. "I don't want to ever go in there again."

"I don't think you have a choice about it," Conrad said— because, of course, the path to Heaven still went through the Memory Pool, whether we liked it or not. Both of us had at least one more jump to go. Hopefully, it was just one.

"There it is!" I called out, seeing the faint glow of the path ahead.

"I can't believe we can see it from way over here," Conrad said. I realized he was right. It was odd to see the glow from so far away.

We proceeded with caution as the path got closer and brighter. We were close enough to see the rocks pulsing. Each stone pulsed with a rhythm similar to that of a resting heartbeat. It was quite cathartic to watch the rocks throb in unison. I felt for my own pulse on my wrist, and when Conrad saw what I was doing, he did the same. We were both amazed. Not only did he and I have the same heart rate, but the rocks were mimicking our pulse beat by beat. We had no idea whether this was good or bad.

Conrad and I aligned, side by side, with our toes just off the path. We held hands. I was on the right, Conrad on the left. The ground was cold under my bare feet, and I noticed that Conrad's boots were gone. When I felt shivers going up my back, I looked down at Conrad's arm and noticed that we had matching goose bumps. The pulse of the rocks began to pound quicker and brighter. I dropped Conrad's hand feeling for my pulse once again. It matched the rhythm of the rocks. It was all so bizarre.

"Take deep breaths with me," I told him. "I want to see whether the pulsing rocks will match us if we calm ourselves down."

I closed my eyes, and Conrad followed suit. Our breathing was in unison: in through the nose and out through the mouth. Our heartbeats slowed.

"Don't open your eyes yet," I told him. "Wait until I tell you to, OK?"

The brief meditation that we performed had such a calming effect on the two of us that we didn't want to come out of it. Eventually, I snapped myself out. I said, "OK, open your eyes on three. One, two, three, open!"

We both opened our eyes to what appeared to be a beautiful surprise. The path was no longer made up of individual rocks. It was a continuous path of fluorescent green pulsation, which was slowly matching our heart rates.

"Whoa, that's gorgeous." Conrad began to feel his heart rate climb and he took a couple of deep breaths to calm down.

"We are meant to be here, for better or worse. You ready?" I looked at Conrad, and he nodded.

The situation was heavy on our minds and our hearts. This was it, the final push forward. All that we had been working toward was right in front of us. The unknown mixed with heightened anticipation created a bevy of emotions for both of us. A tear ran down my right cheek as I envisioned what it might be like to finally put all of this behind me. I saw a happy Todd, Christopher, and Reese along with a safe Ben. I also saw Cliff. I'll always feel at least partially responsible for his rage that night. My affair was the catalyst. I was to blame too, and I knew that.

With each step we took forward, the path beamed under our feet. As long as I'd been here, I had never been able to take more than a few steps without looking over my shoulder to see what was lurking behind me. I felt especially on guard now. I turned my head, glancing over my left shoulder.

"Conrad, stop," I cried out, and I caught hold of his forearm.

"What do you see?"

"Turn your head and take a look behind us."

"Oh my God!" Conrad sounded as if he'd been punched in the gut.

Many times along this journey, I'd convinced myself to push

forward no matter how fearful or unsure I was about what was waiting for me. Never had I felt as helpless as I felt in this moment. The terrain behind us was void of anything. There was absolutely nothing back there but black. It felt like Conrad and I had been locked in a room with no light.

We both turned completely around and stared into this void. I reached my hand out directly in front of me. As my hand became engulfed by the dark, I could feel the temperature quickly drop. I began waving the hand back and forth without being able to see it. Conrad followed my lead, but it was the same for him. It was as if our arms had been chopped off at the elbow.

"They have us," I said.

"Yep, the path forward is all we have now."

It's funny how easy it is to get used to bad situations. Whether it's a bad relationship or an unhealthy lifestyle, somehow, we can fall into the trap of accepting what is. Right now, peering into the dark without being able to see the Memory Pool or Vulture Point in the distance saddened me. I had become accustomed to this uncomfortable place, and now I wondered if I'd ever see it again. And, even more, I wondered why I cared if I did.

Conrad and I turned around, and the pulse of the path we were on picked up with an even brighter glow, as if the path itself knew we were about to continue walking down it. Looking into the distance, I could see an end to the path—an end that looked just as dark as what was behind us. We were now bookended by the dark.

"We must be getting close," Conrad said.

"We are. See!" I pointed to what was the end of the pulsating path.

"Why do you think it stopped pulsing up there?" Conrad asked.

"That must be our final destination. What else could it mean?" My heart raced as we began to march forward again on the path.

As we approached it became clear that, indeed, the path did end. The pulsating glow transformed into a solid glow, which stretched for about thirty yards. This then met a wall of darkness. Conrad and I would have to take a leap of faith into the darkness for our journey to continue.

"We're going to have to get through to the other side," I said. I was confident about moving forward.

"The other side of what?" Conrad was scared. I could hear it in his voice.

"The darkness. There must be something waiting for us on the other side."

"How do you know that?" Of course, Conrad had every right to be skeptical. How could I know that?

"I don't know," I said, "but I don't care. What are our options? We either turn around and step into the darkness behind us, or we keep on going and step into the darkness in front of us. I know which way I'm going, and you're coming with me." I wasn't turning around, and I wouldn't let Conrad do that either.

We arrived at the edge of the path, where the pulsing portion met the solid portion.

"OK, Conrad, it looks like we have another thirty yards or so in front of us before we place our fate in God's hands. Are you ready?" I was surprisingly eager, but that was due to simply not caring anymore.

"Yep, let's do this." Conrad had come around. We were both spent. It was time to put an end to this.

"Just like the Memory Pool, take hold of my hand, and let's go!" I grabbed Conrad's left hand with my right.

We began a light jog, clutching our hands. The last ten yards turned into a full-out sprint. We didn't know whether to jump or just run into the darkness. We chose the latter.

Everything went black. I continued to hold Conrad's hand, but I didn't feel him reciprocating.

"Conrad!" I squeezed his hand harder.

From behind, I was slammed into the ground below. First my knees impacted the strange surface below and then my face. All the while, I gripped Conrad's hand, but still I felt no response from him.

"Conrad, say something!" I screamed in the direction of where I felt his hand. Still no response.

I didn't want to let go of his hand; I was afraid I might lose him forever. I started moving my other hand up Conrad's wrist to his elbow and then to his bicep. I pinched his bicep to no avail. He was unresponsive.

"Once again, Maggie, you have caused harm to someone you care about." The voice came out of the darkness.

"Stay away from me!" I continued to clutch Conrad's hand.

"What are you going to do, Maggie? Really, you have no choice but to listen to me." The voice came closer.

"Conrad!" I grabbed his arm with both of my hands and pulled as hard as I could. I felt like I was in a game of tug o'war.

I abruptly fell back, Conrad in tow. I thought we had collapsed in a heap on the ground, but to my horror, all that fell with me was Conrad's arm from the shoulder down. There was no blood. His arm was cold, like it had been detached for hours.

"Why are you doing this to me?" I shouted in the darkness as I got to my feet, pushing Conrad's lifeless, cold arm off me.

"You've done this to yourself. It's time for you to take responsibility." The voice was closer now.

"Who are you?" I was shivering from fear, not from cold.

"Now, Maggie, I think deep down you know who I am. You just don't want to admit it." The voice was coming from less than two feet away, but it seemed to come from a figure much taller than I was.

And he was right. I knew who he was. I was afraid to accept it. Conrad and I had spent so much energy focused on Marshall, but he was just one of the lieutenants. Cain was the commander-in-chief. He was the one who mattered. My goal had been to find Cain and stop PopCon. Fifty percent of that goal had now been achieved, but I had no plan for how I was going to manage the remaining fifty percent. Of course, I had learned that having a plan here was almost useless. I was a foreigner in a strange land with only my gut instincts to guide me.

As I stared into the darkness toward the direction of Cain's voice, light began to filter in. His face appeared first; eventually the light revealed him from the chest up. He looked gangly. He had slicked back brown hair with some gray scattered throughout. His shoulders were bony and wide. The black shirt he was wearing was raised up awkwardly, leaving a gap from collarbone to collarbone. It was what a T-shirt would look like on a hanger.

"I'm impressed, Maggie," Cain said, speaking with a quiet calm and looking down at me from a height of about six and a half feet. "It's rare that anyone has the nerve to face me. It explains a lot. It reinforces my feelings."

"Reinforces your feelings for what?"

"That you are the right one for us. We've learned to curb our enthusiasm and respect the process before getting too excited, but I had faith. That faith has paid off." Cain gave what could be called a smile but looked more like a cocky smirk.

"I'm not the right one for you," I said with authority. "And I never will be. You're evil, and the day is coming where you'll no longer be able to torture the living or the dead." I looked directly into Cain's eyes as I spoke.

"Oh Maggie, your blind ambition has failed you. You don't know why you're here, do you?" Cain's smirk turned into a full smile.

While there had been times during this journey when I had confidently felt I could carry out the Gateway's mission, reality hit me once I truly saw Cain. He looked formidable. This journey was, and has always been about a reckoning for me and my family. I understood that this might sound selfish—and probably *was* selfish—but that's all I'd ever cared about. I would carry my guilt eternally, but if I could right a wrong here with Cain, I would feel that I'd accomplished my mission to save my loved ones from the consequences of my mistakes.

It wasn't easy to muster the courage. Through trembling lips, I told Cain, "I'm here to protect my family from you."

He smiled again. "Nathan and Nigel are laughing at you right now. They've tasked you with an impossible mission. You aren't their first pawn, and you won't be their last. But for me, you are a welcome sight."

The anger I felt inside was balanced with curiosity. Why was I a welcome sight?

Cain continued, "I can't speak for Cliff, but I can assure you that Ben is in good hands." He raised one lanky arm into the air and called out, "Ben!"

I could hear footsteps approaching from behind Cain. "Ben," I said, speaking almost in a whisper. "Are you here?" I felt faint as the footsteps drew nearer.

From the darkness my boy appeared. I smiled, but Ben did not smile in return. My heart skipped a beat as my son came to a stop beside Cain.

Cain spoke first. "Maggie, we thank you for delivering Ben to us."

I was mentally drained, both cold and scared. Cain's words made no sense to me.

Speaking directly to Ben, I asked, "What have they done to you?" I reached a hand out to him, but I wasn't close enough to touch him, and he stood next to Cain with his arms crossed impeccably over his chest. There seemed to be no way in.

I said, "You're scaring me, Ben. Please stop."

At that, Ben came to life. He pointed his index finger at me, waving it just six inches away from my face. "I'm *scaring* you?" he shouted. "Scaring *you?*"

"Yes, please stop. And tell me, why are you here?"

He let his hand drop, but he was still glaring at me. "I'm here because of you! You did this."

I fell back, feeling as if my son had struck me with his words. The weight of everything I'd been through came crashing down on me. I was weeping silently, and through my tears, I once again tried to reach out to Ben. He backed up an inch or two, and it looked like he shuddered. He wanted nothing to do with me, and he remained by Cain's side.

Cain spoke once again. "Maggie, I know you've been trying to figure out why you're here and not in Heaven." Cain paused and glanced at Ben, then came back to me.

"I know why I'm here," I said, wiping the tears from my face. "I'm here to stop you."

"No, Maggie, not at all," Cain said, grinning again. "You came to help me. Because of you, I can rest in peace, knowing I have passed on PopCon's leadership to a capable and strong individual—someone you created and, through your actions, delivered to us."

Like a proud parent, Cain placed a hand on Ben's shoulder, and said, "So, thank you, Maggie, for your priceless gift."

I felt violated and humiliated. I'd thought I might be a pawn for Gateway, but instead I'd been a pawn for PopCon. Their evil master plan had been executed flawlessly, and I, unknowingly, had played a crucial role.

I turned back to my son. "Ben, this is not you," I told him. "Please don't fall into PopCon's trap. Do you know what they do here? They manipulate people and take their lives. They destroy hope. They *killed* me."

"That's an interesting theory," Ben said, "but you have your facts wrong. PopCon didn't kill you. How could they have done that? Look into my eyes, and tell me what you see."

Ben was glowering straight into my eyes, and as I looked back into his, I realized that I didn't recognize my son. Those eyes boring into mine did not belong to the boy I had raised.

Still, what could I say? I told him, "I see a confused young man— a manipulated young man. I see my son desperately trying to get out." My eyes welled with tears again.

"Wrong again. Look deeper and you'll see it. You'll see the person who ended your life. That's right, fifty-three blows—fifty-three fucking hits with that hammer. And you deserved another fifty-three, you selfish bitch." Ben didn't raise his voice. He didn't have to.

"So, Maggie, things are never as they seem, are they?" Cain was brimming with pride in his protégé and successor.

"It's time for you to leave," Ben told me. "You may see us again; you may not. Just know that you did this. You ruined our family, and I decided to ruin you. Even Dad knew I did the right thing. That's why he is sitting in jail for the rest of his life. He protected me, always. You protected yourself, and look where you are now. There's a place in Hell waiting for you. So, you know where to go. Just get the fuck out of here!" Ben turned around and walked back into the darkness with Cain.

I fell to my knees, hands over my eyes, and cried harder than I had ever cried before. The son I had loved so much was gone. He left us that fateful night when he embarked on his path of destruction. Actions always have consequences, but the consequences of these actions might be eternal. Perhaps Ben's destiny had been set into motion before my affair with Brent, but I had to shoulder at least some of the blame. My husband was in jail for a crime he'd confessed to but hadn't committed— the ultimate sacrifice to protect his guilty son. Ben's siblings—Reese, Todd, and Christopher—might be in Heaven, but they'd had their lives cut short, and they'd been robbed of making memories of their own.

As for me, my punishment seemed to be never ending. It occurred to me that looks could be deceiving. Maybe this *was* Hell.

Was there a way out? Was there anything I could do to recompense for the harm I had caused? I knew that I wanted to rise up and fight for *all* of my children!

Look for the next book in the series:

The Vulture Rises

ABOUT THE AUTHOR

Chris Gallagher has worked on the business side of sports and entertainment for twenty-five years, associated with such teams as the New York Yankees, the Cleveland Browns, and the Miami Dolphins. Chris enjoys a good sporting event—and he also enjoys a good story, which is what led him to the thrilling world of fantasy fiction. When Chris isn't working, he writes tales he can share with his wife and son and a growing number of fans. He lives with his family in Windermere, Florida.